Love is
a time of enchantment:
in it all days are fair and all fields
green. Youth is blest by it,
old age made benign: the eyes of love see
roses blooming in December,
and sunshine through rain. Verily
is the time of true-love
a time of enchantment — and
Oh! how eager is woman
to be bewitched!

VOLLANDS

Following her husband's bankruptcy, Anna Volland accepts the offer of hospitality from her Uncle Hubert, and takes her large family to live at 'Vollands'. Hubert's death leaves 'Vollands' in the hands of James, her cold and business-like son, whose treatment of Jenny, Hubert's daughter, brings tragedy to her and to the family.

PAMELA HILL

VOLLANDS

Complete and Unabridged

ULVERSCROFT
Leicester

First published in Great Britain in 1990 by
Robert Hale Limited, London

First Large Print Edition
published January 1992
by arrangement with
Robert Hale Limited, London

British Library CIP Data

Hill, Pamela, *1920–*
    Vollands. — Large print ed. —
    Ulverscroft large print series: romance
    I. Title
    823.914 [F]

ISBN 0–7089–2577–4

Published by
F. A. Thorpe (Publishing) Ltd.
Anstey, Leicestershire

Set by Words & Graphics Ltd.
Anstey, Leicestershire
Printed and bound in Great Britain by
T. J. Press (Padstow) Ltd., Padstow, Cornwall

Part One

1

ANNA VOLLAND lay on her chaise-longue, with a light woollen cover, dutifully crocheted by her eldest daughter Christian, draped over her elegant feet. Christian was making another now, jabbing with her large white hands at the work as she coaxed the hook in and out of the odds and ends of coloured wool. She sat bolt upright to perform this task, as if to deny her statuesque beauty any poise or grace. Anna, watching, reflected ironically that it no longer mattered; Christian was twenty-eight, and could no longer be expected to marry even had there not been the necessity, incumbent on eldest daughters, of looking after her mother. In case she had had to consider herself selfish, Anna consoled herself with the assurance that Christian had never seemed interested in marriage. Her mind had for some years seemed totally occupied by her correspondence with Dr Arnold, the headmaster of Rugby school, who sent improving precepts to Christian by letter and received grateful answers by return. But, Anna reflected somewhat spitefully, Dr Arnold was married, with a large and increasing family; there was no hope there.

She returned her brilliant hazel gaze from her daughter to the young neighbour who had, as happened almost daily, disposed himself at her feet the better to pour out his adoration. Anna knew her own age, which was fifty; she also knew that young Handley would never escape from the grip of his widowed mother, who did not call at Vollands. There were reasons for that; poor Henry's bankruptcy, which in the end had killed him —

" — and no other woman can compare with you; I have seen them all, in London and in Paris. You are like a jewel buried in the sand, here at Vollands."

"Dear young man, I choose to bury myself so that I may select my company." She smiled brilliantly on him; her teeth were still good; if she looked in a glass what she saw did not offend her. She spent little time in caring for her beauty;

now that they could no longer keep a stable of hunters she went for a brisk walk every morning, with one or more daughters to accompany her; that was all.

Mr Handley transferred his worshipping gaze from her face to her hair; Volland hair, Anna's especial beauty; silver-gilt in colour and piled high regardless of fashion, which demanded low-swept curls at present. The Vollands — Anna had married her cousin, to her parents' displeasure — had Viking blood, and every few generations this silver-fair colouring came out, in Anna's case redeemed by darker brows and lashes. Philippa, the second daughter, and little Mark had light ones. As for Hew, the elder twin, he was as dark as Satan, and so had Harry been, judging from his portrait, before he broke his neck in a hunting accident. Octavia was dark too, with rosy cheeks, a taking little thing; on the other hand nobody liked James, who was fair, with a mean narrow face and prim mouth. As for Buckland, the other twin, he never said a word. One had almost forgotten Juley; her hair was glossy brown. The family fascinated Handley, but at a distance; he was completely taken up with their mother.

Anna had meantime wearied of polite talk and surveyed the drawing-room from beneath her lashes. There were portraits hung about the walls, most of them the property of her uncle Hubert Volland, who owned this house. They had a gloomy appearance, almost a blight, even Harry's, painted in a pink coat at his coming-of-age and completed just before his death five years back. The room suffered from damp like the rest of the house, but as they were permitted by Uncle Hubert to live here for no rent, and had coal and wood supplied, it would have been ungracious to complain. The old gentleman himself had been able, before their coming, to move himself, his belongings and his many bastards, wife, mistress and two legitimate daughters up the hill to his almost completed seat of Hubertshall, a mighty abode with a gilded ship spinning with the wind on top of the central tower. This was in acknowledgment of Uncle Hubert's brief service in the Navy in his youth with the Duke of Clarence, lately King. Vollands had become the dower-house, and they were lucky to get it; lucky also in that Uncle Hubert had been involved very lightly in poor Henry's financial disaster. How like Henry — one could think of it without disloyalty — that his own venture into speculation, made partly for her sake, should have ended in abject failure and bankruptcy! "I want to buy you silk dresses, diamonds, furs, the things rich women have who are not half as beautiful as you," he had murmured against her. Dear Henry; she had after all been faithful to him and had borne him nine children. The end had been sad; she turned her head away. Young Handley was saying something; one had best listen.

She suddenly focused her gaze on Handley's face and noted, not for the first time, that he was not unlike her late husband; Henry had had the same dark hair, blunt features, and dog-like devotion in his eyes. If only Henry could occasionally have been successful at anything except making children! Her mother had warned her. "He will never come to anything.

You have made your bed and you must lie on it." That had been when Christian, correct upright Christian, had been conceived before the marriage; they had been unable to wait, and it had forced her parents' hand. "Nowadays it would not have been alluded to," murmured Anna; times were stricter than they had been in Prinny's day.

At the sound of her voice Handley looked up. How beautiful she was, he thought; no other woman he knew, no young woman, could compare with her. That fine profile like Diana's; the curve of her lips, wistful and yet fanciful! It drove a man mad, and yet not with thoughts of marriage; she was a goddess on a pedestal, forever inviolate. His mama, who held the purse-strings, had been forthright. "The widow of a bankrupt! The mother of nine! My son, I wonder at you." Often he wondered at himself, but could not be free of the enchantment of Anna Volland. Tillotson, the other admirer, an old maid of a fellow, was the same; often they would come and sit together, gazing and listening.

Anna had forgotten him again and was

gazing at the portrait of her dead son Harry, in his pink coat. His handsome head was held high, as if daring the jump that had killed him. He had been afraid of nothing, from a child; Hew resembled him in ways, but was younger. She could have used Harry's courage in the year that he had died; it had been then also that Henry, the venture having failed, had shot himself in the billiard-room of their old home. Left desolate, they had come to Vollands by invitation of Uncle Hubert. It was like Henry to have left no portrait of himself to bring, only a little miniature in a gilt frame which one could hardly see from here. It was as though his memory had shrunk in importance to such a size; in fact, she did not often think of him. One must not dwell on the past; it was gone. There were the children, eight of them, remaining; no doubt they would come in for tea.

Tea was brought, the raw country girl who was all they could afford to employ carrying the tray in her red hands carefully. On it reposed, beside the silver teapot Uncle Hubert had rescued from the sale of their goods, a beautifully iced cake. This was the work of Philippa, who to her mother's dismay preferred spending her time in the kitchen to doing the things young ladies ought to do. Despite the light eyelashes Pippa was pretty, but seldom seen without an apron; a Christmas gift some years ago of Miss Moxon's cookery book had proved a disaster. Ladies did not, Anna told her daughter, bake, decorate cakes and concoct iced puddings; however, provided no coarser ventures such as basting a roast of meat were undertaken, Pippa might pass her time as she chose; and certainly everyone enjoyed eating what she made. She would appear presently, having washed her hands and taken off her apron. Meantime Anna commenced the pouring of tea before it grew cold; if her family were late it was their own fault.

"Here are Hew and Buckland, Mama," said Christian quietly. She had laid aside her crochet, and as the young servant had departed, rose and went herself to open the door to her brothers.

They came nonchalantly lounging in, tall and fresh from their day's shooting.

Buckland's thick fair hair was all of a tangle, Hew's black locks wind-blown about his handsome wedge of a face with its hawk's nose and bright eyes, dark as a bird's. Anna poured their tea and Christian handed it to them. They drank it standing, Buckland with a particular eye on the cake.

"That looks good, Mama," said Hew, as his twin was silent. "May we cut it?"

"I suppose that you may, if you offer a piece to Mr Handley. What did you bag today?" Whatever they had shot would have to do for supper in three, four days, when it had had time to hang.

"A partridge, a brace of widgeon, a couple of hares," replied Hew, munching. Buckland, who was a better shot than his brother, claimed no credit; his constant refuge was silence. He stood some way behind Hew as was his custom, having received his piece of cake. Both young men were hungry; presently they reached for a second slice.

"I can tell you who we saw, driving past," Hew remarked through the crumbs. "Uncle Hubert's Eliza. She was with a soldier, and had her bonnet on." He grinned.

Christian primmed up her mouth. Dr Arnold, her beloved correspondent, would be the last to approve of the lax morals prevailing up the hill and discussed openly and often by her family. Uncle Hubert, as the whole county knew, had made a young maid-servant his mistress years ago when she first came, shortly after his second marriage. By now he had several children by her. Other families did not admit to this kind of situation, let alone permit it to thrive in their midst. If it should happen, they referred to it, if at all, as a misfortune and otherwise kept quiet about it. There was nobody, granted, as colourful as Uncle Hubert, who seemed left over from a previous age; and had two dull daughters by two dull wives, and plenty of sons by Eliza.

Anna was smiling a little. "Uncle Hubert will not be pleased if Eliza has run off."

"She hardly needs another lover," remarked Hew. Christian gave a shocked exclamation. "Remember," she said, "that you are in the presence of Mama."

He was prevented from replying by the entry of Pippa, the younger sisters Juley and Octavia, and little Mark, who had been born only two years before Henry's death and remembered nothing but life at Vollands. Christian at once seized him by the hand as if to protect him from the prevailing naughty talk, but the small boy wrenched away.

"I want cake," he said firmly, and marched to the tray. Pippa laughed, and cut him a slice. His Volland hair was still almost white, his brows and lashes like an albino's. Octavia, dark and rosy-cheeked, just overtopped him; she would never be tall. She wore, as all the sisters had to wear in turn, the cast-offs, made down to size, of her elders. There was hardly any cake left for her, and she said so.

"You should have come earlier," Anna replied. The hazel eyes regarded her assembled family without affection or much interest. They would lead their own lives, as she had led hers. They had meant trouble in giving them birth, but that was finished with. She returned her attention to Mr Handley, the admiring neighbour.

"I fear my brood have eaten everything up like a plague of locusts," she said. "Will you take more tea?"

It was worth encouraging him; he might do, sooner or later, for one of the girls, in spite of his mother.

James Volland, the eldest son now Harry was dead, had not come in to tea; he regarded it as a frivolous institution. His mother encountered him later, when he had shut the door of his study and left his accounts behind; James was forever closeted with accounts. Anna twitted him about it. He answered her gravely, his small mouth pursing under its fair moustache.

"If I am ever to attain some position in the county, Mama, it is necessary to clear off my late father's debts."

"Your great-uncle Hubert could not manage that, and you will not. Why not enjoy yourself a little, like your brothers?"

"My brothers lead an idle and useless existence. I am disinclined to imitate them."

Anna shrugged; he was so pleased with himself there was no doing anything with

14

him. She could not imagine whence came this smugness; neither her own branch of the family nor his father's had it. She glanced up, again, at the portraits, and happened on the one of her mother, fair-haired also and with a discontented expression; she had not been happy in her own marriage, forced into it at seventeen. Nevertheless she had wanted to arrange another match for Anna than the one she herself had chosen with Henry, for love. Perhaps the human race never learnt anything.

"You are not listening to me, Mama," complained James.

They were interrupted by the approaching thunder of hooves, which stopped abruptly outside. Anna stayed where she was and made no change in her expression; James stiffened a little, like a private whose commanding officer makes known his impending presence. Both of them knew what the noise meant; the arrival of Uncle Hubert.

He strode into the room, a huge man well over six feet tall; his indulgence since youth in beer and wine had given him a formidable stomach, which he carried

15

before him with pride. His Volland hair had long ago turned white, but sprang back from his brow with such vigour that it seemed like that of a young man, and showed no signs of thinning. Nothing about him, in fact, gave any indication of old age, yet he was in his seventies, and let everyone know it: in fact, he let everyone know everything, and now, without greeting his niece or her eldest son, he launched forth in a diatribe of grief and rage; his mistress had run off with a common soldier.

"After all I'd done for her; bought her a silk gown only last week. Took her to town and bought it. We went to the theatre. Eliza hadn't been in a theatre before, wasn't used to that kind of thing. When I think of what she was when she came, and what I made her into — "

He raved on, and Anna and James were for once thinking the same thing; Eliza Bowling had been a little maid who had been hired to dust and clean, an orphan who had nobody to look after her. Hubert Volland had taken an unaccountable lust to her, had put her in his bed and kept her there, while his wife languished alone in her rooms. In ten years Eliza had borne her master eight children, and had grown accustomed to the use of rosewater on her skin, fine underwear, and drives in the carriage. What had caused her to elope with the soldier nobody knew, unless it was that Eliza had tired of constant pregnancies and wished to withdraw among her own kind.

"She'll find a difference," sniffed Hubert. He glared round the room. "Edith and the girls are followin' in the phaeton."

"You have not dragged poor Aunt Edith into this?" said Anna, speaking for the first time. Uncle Hubert blew out his moustaches.

"Why not, pray?" he said. "She — Eliza — hadn't the common courage to tell me herself that she was goin', and can't write, of course: so she told little Jenny, our eldest, and Jenny told me, afterwards, that is. That child's pure gold, shy as she is. Ellen and Maud can't do without her. They're all comin' down with one another."

James pulled himself together sufficiently to ask his great-uncle if he would take wine. Hubert had never been known to refuse it, and they were all three drinking placidly when the phaeton drew up outside the door, making a discreet sound with its wheels on the pebbles. Four ladies debouched from its open interior, the eldest with her face almost concealed by a bonnet and symmetrical bunches of curled hair dyed black. This was Edith Volland, Hubert's second wife, crushed by him from the beginning and hardly ever known to say anything. She had produced one daughter, Ellen, so like her half-sister Maud, the fruit of the first marriage, that they were often mistaken for one another; both had thin flaxen hair, invisible eyebrows, and bad teeth. They had lived a twilight existence in the Hubertshall tower with Edith while their bastard half-brothers and sisters romped below. Whether the situation would now change remained to be seen; but it was at least significant that the legitimate family had today been permitted to occupy the phaeton.

The ladies arranged themselves on lesser sofas and chairs. Anna remained where she was; it was a tradition that she did not rise to her feet for anybody. Edith was persuaded to accept a small glass of ratafia. The girls took nothing. Suddenly James spoke up, addressing bastard Jenny, the youngest present.

"Will you not try a little of Pippa's lemonade?" he said courteously. "It is really very good, and freshly brewed."

Jenny smiled shyly up at him. By contrast to her half-sisters she was an enchanting sight, possibly resembling her mother when she had first ensnared Uncle Hubert, but quieter. Jenny's hair was golden; not the silver-gilt of the Vollands, but the gold of ripe corn, of Ceres. She was plainly dressed and her gown, with its close-fitting bodice, showed her to be still part child, yet almost woman. She held herself gracefully, however she had learned to do so; and her mouth was so fashioned that it seemed to be smiling even when her face was still. She was the loveliest thing that had been seen in that drawing-room since the coming of Anna; and in her different way, in her shy promise, she excelled her, though she hardly ever spoke for shyness. Anna, naturally, was not too pleased;

but she ordered the lemonade, and in the end Ellen and Maud drank some too, even exclaiming at its excellence. However Hubert spoke up, and silenced everybody.

"I mean to do what I can for my sister's family," he announced. "I remember y'mother, niece; fine figure of a woman, but got downhearted. She liked to dress up for church; it was the only solace she had."

"There were Paul and myself, Uncle Hubert," said Anna plaintively.

"Well, Paul's done for himself by marryin' that Spaniard and fatherin' a brood of Papists in Malaga: he can mind his own affairs. You, my dear, are different; I'll see your daughters married if I can, and I'll do what I may for your sons. You," he turned to James, "have the makin's of a man of business; God knows you're always at it. If you had capital, might make somethin' of it; better than y'father, more sense."

James gave his narrow smile. "It is easy to speculate, uncle, because I have none. The fact hinders me considerably."

"I dare say, I dare say. I will advance

a certain sum on one condition; do you agree?"

"I cannot agree until I know what the condition is, uncle."

"Wisely put. If you will take your pick of one or other of these two damned ugly daughters of mine, takin' one off my hands, I'll see you started in whatever venture you prefer. I'm a warm man, as they say; I'd intended leavin' everythin' to Eliza for our family, but now they can go to the devil. They're a servant's children, and may take a servant's place."

"Really, Hubert, is that kind?"

Edith had spoken at last. He looked at her as if she were some curious animal. "What have you to say to anythin'?" he asked her. "They're none of 'em yours."

She began to weep, blotting her tears with a lace-edged handkerchief. Nobody else said anything. Anna lay on her chaise-longue in silent amusement, as if she were watching a play. Hubert's elder daughters sat side by side, expressionless as two eggs. James's jaw had dropped a little. How different, he was thinking, if he had been offered pretty Jenny!

"Well?" said Uncle Hubert. "Which of

'em do you want, or neither? If it's neither I wouldn't blame you. If I wasn't damned certain their two mothers never got out, I would think they weren't mine. But there it is, and I have to provide for 'em. Which is it to be? Maud or Ellen? Ellen or Maud? Damned if I know which is which."

James bowed, and said that he would leave it to his uncle's discretion to pick him a bride. In the end Maud was chosen, as the elder. Like her stepmother, she burst into tears, and begged that Jenny might stay with her when she came to live at Vollands. At that, Ellen objected; she wanted Jenny to stay with her at Hubertshall. Suddenly, Anna intervened.

"If all Eliza's children are to be sent out to earn their living, it is as well if Jenny stays with us," she said. Her purpose in saying this was not very clear to her, except that it would please James.

Hew and Buckland waylaid the old man as he was about to mount his horse; they had by some means heard that he was disposed to be beneficent to the family.

At first, he glared at them; what the devil did they want?

"Commissions in the Hussars, Uncle Herbert," said Hew in his forthright way. Buckland, as usual, said nothing. Hubert Volland stared.

"You'd drink yourselves stupid in the mess and run up debt. There's no war at present."

"When it comes, we'd be ready," said Hew. As far as his features could assume a beseeching expression, they did so; but meantime the old man had adopted an almost devilish aspect.

"Write me, the pair of you, an application in Latin, and I'll consider it. I doubt if either of you has ever paid heed to anything a tutor taught you, all your days."

He rode off, and Hew looked at Buckland and they grinned at each other. They knew very well that they would obtain their heart's desire.

2

"THEY say the two middle brothers have ridden off to the army, with old Squire Hubert's blessing," said Lady Yester, lifting her satin-clad elbow. Since the exigencies of being her late husband's wife while he was on George IV's Privy Council, she had acquired the habit of taking a little brandy and water when not in company. Mrs Lannoy, her nearest neighbour, could hardly be called even that; the two of them met almost daily to gossip, and continued to surprise one another at how much material there was available in this remote corner of England.

Mrs Lannoy sipped her own brandy. It would have been churlish to dear Lady Yester to refuse it, although one still felt that it was not quite a lady's drink. To elevate her mind above such considerations she replied with whatever information she had acquired about the Volland family. Squire Volland was, of

24

course, quite disreputable, and behaved like an eighteenth-century version of himself when in church, shouting down the parson, or else falling asleep in the middle of the sermon and snoring loudly till it was finished. As for his brood of children, it was not respectable even to mention those, although they somehow packed themselves each week into a pew. Now that the mother had taken herself off, nobody knew what would happen, and perhaps whatever did would be for the best. The niece, Mrs Anna Volland, of course came very seldom to church, and when she did so swept in like a queen, as if someone ought to be present to hold her train. Her children — "I have been thinking about those daughters," said Lady Yester. "They are left alone now that the brothers have gone, except for James."

Mrs Lannoy surveyed her half-empty glass. James Volland was the only member of his family who troubled to attend church regularly, and he had recently been put forward as a possible vestryman, but the suggestion had been turned down because of his origins. If anyone had known the fury with which James had received the news of his rejection, they would certainly have blenched; but being prudent, and with an eye to the future, James had said nothing about it openly.

"The daughters," Mrs Lannoy echoed. "If the mother had taken the least trouble to ensure it, the eldest — Christian, is it not? — would have been married long ago, with those looks. As for the rest, I know very little."

"Christian is what we used to call a bluestocking," said Lady Yester, "and may not be suited to marriage. But the others are mannerly girls. I am considering sending them an invitation to Olivia's summer party." Olivia was her niece.

"That will be kind," admitted Mrs Lannoy. "It is some years since the bankruptcy."

"Which was not their fault. I rather think it may have been their mother's; the husband they say was besotted with her, and did whatever she said."

"Will you invite Mrs Anna?"

"No, nor Christian. It is a young people's occasion. The younger girls,

Philippa, Julia, Octavia, and little Mark, shall come."

The invitation-card arrived, and was given pride of place on the Vollands mantel in what had been used to be called the schoolroom, but only Christian ever now taught anyone anything there. Governesses had been tried in their time and had failed, mostly because their charges endorsed one another in the denial of whatever happened to be under discussion, leaving Africa in America, and kangaroos in the Middle West. Christian, on the other hand, was dull and prosy; imparting, or trying to, whatever Dr Arnold sent her: but there was no Sixth Form here to take charge of all the rest of the school according to his new method, and her mother, when appealed to, refused to take the least interest in whatever might be fermenting in the minds of her children.

"Mama, Mark ought to be made ready for a preparatory school, which would bring him on for later education such as he might receive at Rugby."

"My dear girl, do not set your cap at

the headmaster of Rugby; he has a wife and almost as many children as Uncle Hubert."

Christian flushed. "Mama, it is not a question of setting one's cap; that would be very vulgar."

"Then of what is it a question?" Anna raised a delicate white hand and yawned behind it. Christian bridled a little; everything Mama did was graceful when it ought to be disgraceful, like yawning in public.

"It is a matter of exchanging ideas," she stated piously. Anna turned her silver-gilt head and smiled.

"Ah," was all she replied. At that moment a neighbour was announced who often came; not Mr Handley today, but Mr Tillotson, with his long nose and prim ways. They were all the same, nevertheless, in essentials, these young men: in their thirties, of sufficient fortune, endowed with manly attributes, and prepared to adore, but only Mama; there was so far no question of marrying any of her daughters.

The lawns of Lady Yester's house had been scythed close, the shrubberies swept, the trees themselves trimmed of any unsightly lower branches. It had been intended to put up a great tent on the scythed grass, and lay out the refreshments there to be brought out as required and eaten *al fresco*. Everything was prepared for the great day, even the jugs of cider-cup standing ready in the ice-house to keep cool; when down came the rain. It rained in torrents, putting paid to any notion that might have been had of outdoor games and races of a kind suitable both for young ladies and young gentlemen. There was nothing for it but to withdraw the party inside the house, and re-arrange the refreshments in the dining-room, while a fiddler was hastily hired to play for quadrilles in the drawing-room.

Miss Olivia, a pretty dark-haired girl of twelve, took the disappointment placidly; the weather would make no difference to the fact that she could wear her new pale-blue gown with a rolled hem, which suited her admirably and was the very latest fashion from Paris. She stood to receive her soaked young guests with aplomb, and presently led off Oranges and Lemons to the tune of the fiddler, to dry everyone up. The elegant room was filled with pleasant noise, music, and chatter. Very few grown-ups were there.

Pippa, Juley, Octavia and Mark had arrived late, due to the breakdown of their ancient trap. Its leather hood had prevented the ruin of their dresses, and had saved an offering Pippa still held and had meant to give to Olivia had the latter not been too greatly taken up with what she was at. It was a plateful of dainty sweets in different colours, made of marzipan, fondant, cherries and nuts. Pippa held it a little self-consciously, not knowing whether to keep it or to put it down. The other three were not interested; Juley had transformed herself with a fall of their mother's lace, worn Spanish fashion, and looked very pretty; Ocky was as usual watching everybody in a sly way beneath her hair; and Mark hated parties and was looking for some other boy with whom to fight.

Suddenly Pippa's dilemma was resolved. A friendly voice said in her ear: "I say, those look good, better than most things here. Where d'you get 'em?"

"I made them," said Pippa. The young

man to whom she spoke widened his very blue eyes in admiration, whether of herself or of the sweets was not yet clear.

"I say!" It was the second time he had said it; Ocky would have told him so, but Pippa was too kind-hearted. In fact he was not a child, hardly a boy either, more of a young man; almost too old for the party; perhaps almost twenty. He had red hair, a freckled skin, a snub nose, and the sea-blue eyes she had already noted. He was very tall. Pippa found herself smiling at him. She was not a stranger to young men; apart from Mama's admirers, there were her brothers.

"You can eat some if you like," she told him. "I brought them for Olivia, but she's busy."

He chose a green one, then a cherry one, then a vanilla. "What else," he asked, munching, "do you make? My name is Martin Fielding. I'm Olivia's cousin."

"Mine is Philippa Volland." As she said it she flushed a little; people, when they heard the name of Volland, often turned away. But this nice boy stayed with her, and it wasn't only the sweets; he didn't

31

take any more of those. He asked what else she made.

"Cakes, ices, all kinds of things. Mama doesn't like me to cook properly; she says it isn't ladylike."

"I'd say it's worth being unladylike if everything you make is as good as those were. Olivia! Come here! You're missing the best part of your day. Look what Miss Volland has brought you, and I've eaten three of 'em."

Why thirty generations of landlubberly squires should have produced a young man with a passion for the sea mystified, at least, the present Squire Fielding, a widower with no ambition to marry again. When Martin, at the age of twelve, had declared his intention of joining the Navy, his father had not forbidden it; that would have been the surest way to make the boy run off. Instead, and with native cunning, the Squire had represented himself as a lone figure, with nobody but his only son to look to when he grew old; nobody to care about the estates in his absence but bailiffs; and so on, until Martin, who had a soft heart, allowed himself to be persuaded to stay at home, learn about managing the estates, and in general become the prop of his father's not very apparent old age. He still hankered after the sea, took every chance of sailing on it that he could, and was glad and proud that King William IV had once been a sailor. That was as far as it might ever go; he had accepted his own lot, which was not a bad one. In return, his father let him have his way in everything else; and it says a good deal for Martin's sweetness that he did not grow up spoilt.

Nevertheless, when he walked into the Squire's study the day after Olivia's party and announced that he had found his bride, all was not smooth upon the waters: especially when it turned out that the young lady's surname was Volland.

"One o' those! Thieves and vagabonds! The old uncle put a kitchen wench in his bed and left his wife upstairs, and they had God knows how many — The gel ain't one o' *those*?"

"It would not signify if she were, Papa, but in fact she is the daughter of no kitchen wench. Her parents were respectably married. Her father is dead. I ascertained as much as that. Recollect that we only met yesterday."

"You put the question to a gel you only met yesterday? It's as well I'm here; at this rate I shan't be here long."

Martin's blue eyes twinkled. "Come, Papa, you have been prophesying your demise ever since I was a small boy. I heeded you then, but now — "

"Well, what now? Remember you ain't of age; can't go marryin' lightskirt wenches anyhow."

Martin's mouth set; he suddenly looked much older. "Kindly do not miscall Philippa, sir, or by God I will join the Navy and take her with me to wives' quarters."

"Are you certain she'd go?" demanded his father with instant shrewdness. The guard came down between them and Martin smiled.

"I am certain of nothing, except that she is the girl for me. I have not, as you ask, put the question yet; for her sake — she is very young — it would be best if I were to make myself known to her family, then declare myself. I am surprised no other man has done so; Pippa is an excellent baker and confectioner. You have a sweet tooth, sir; you will like to have her here."

"You seem determined, at any rate," grumbled the Squire, half persuaded. "I'd better take a look at her. I'll ask Hattie Yester."

Lady Yester had, long before the party invitation to the girls, left cards on Anna Volland as she considered to be her Christian duty, but she had not entered the house. Now, at the earnest persuasion of her old friend Tom Fielding, she agreed to do so, and they drove over with Martin in the carriage. On the way Pippa was tactfully not mentioned, but they talked about Anna.

"Never seen her," said the Squire, who lived across the shire border and went to a different parish church.

"Very few persons have, unless they visit her," Lady Yester replied. "She is one of those people to whom the world comes, but who do not go to the world."

"Her world seems made up of young

men, I hear. Be careful of yourself, Martin; may find y'self caught up with the old lady instead of the young."

Martin had the dignity not to reply, and continued gazing out of the window. Vollands came in sight at last, foursquare among its trees, painted a pearly grey that was beginning to crumble and flake. It had been built just after the Civil Wars, when its then owner had returned from abroad with the King to find his old home razed, and accordingly constructed a new one. It had a graceful French influence and arches, like eyebrows, decorating the outer walls. Seen closely, the roof needed mending.

The red-handed little maid who the other day had brought in tea admitted them; she, and the man who scythed the grass, were the only servants. The arrivals found the drawing-room full; both Mr Tillotson and Mr Handley were in attendance, and as both were known to all it made for free and easy talk. Anna lay on her chaise-longue, and extended her graceful white hand. Christian, who was in attendance nearby, rose from where she had been sitting, and acknowledged the new acquaintances in her stately way. Mark lay on the threadbare carpet, drawing on wrapping-paper; he took no notice of anybody. There was no sign of Pippa.

Lady Yester, being a woman of the world, did not take long to realise that her old friend Tom Fielding was, as the vulgar say, struck all of a heap. Like many men before him, he gazed at Anna with his mouth half open, and no sound emerging: when invited to sit by her, he did so with the clumping lack of grace of a great schoolboy, perching at last on the frail chair, with his hands planted on his knees. Whatever Anna was saying to him was not audible, but the two young men in attendance heard; laughed, as if it was the wittiest thing in the world, and gazed adoringly at its perpetrator. Lady Yester watched, not unamused, but aware that she herself was being left to her own devices. She was also aware, looking round, that Martin had disappeared.

Martin, possessing the sense of direction which would have enabled him to steer a ship by the North Star, knew that the kitchens of a house were at the back, down flights of stairs, and along stone passages. Accordingly, he made his way towards where these might be expected to find themselves; opened a door, and beheld two young women, one almost a child, sewing baby-clothes. Anyone less lovelorn than Martin would have noted the beauty of young Jenny, with the sunlight shining on her corn-gold hair; but she mattered nothing, and neither did the other, older, colourless young woman who was also plying a needle. In other words, James had coldly done his duty by Maud, who was in the family way after three months of marriage, and wretchedly sick, wishing herself back in the tower with Mama and Ellen. Jenny had hesitantly mentioned diapers; her own Mama used to sew dozens of them, and they had better get a great many ready because they needed washing all the time. Maud retched, and Martin, who had been about to ask where the kitchens were, hastily withdrew.

He blundered next into the schoolroom, where Juley and Octavia were wrestling with household accounts served on them lately by Christian, who said they ought to learn to understand such things. The two heads, one brown, one dark, were close together over the problem. When Martin cleared his throat neither girl had the manners to rise.

"It's you," said Juley, who remembered him from the party. "What d'you want?" She was at the ungracious age, often awkward, sometimes bewitching; in time, she would be the beauty of the family, but at present she was too thin.

"I want to know the way to the kitchen," he told them in downright fashion. It had never occurred to him that Pippa could be anywhere else, and he was not going to mention her in front of these two children.

However, Ocky spoke up. "You want Pippa," she said. "She's making pastry. Down there."

She jumped from her place, a rosy-cheeked fairy, and ran in front of Martin to show him the way he ought to go. To his relief, she did not come with him. At last he found Pippa in a vast stone-lined place, rolling out buttered dough, a lock of fair hair fallen forwards over her flushed face. Several skinned rabbits in vinegar lay in dishes nearby, and a fire blazed to heat the oven, making the kitchen like a furnace.

There were trimmings from the pastry, and Martin took one in his fingers and ate it. At that she looked round and saw him, and smiled. "Oh!" she said. "I thought you were one of the children."

He was pleased; there was no coyness here, only liking; she was the most natural girl he had ever met. "It isn't good for you raw," she added, as he prepared to steal another trimming. The blue eyes were watching her steadily.

"Good for me or not, it is delicious," he told her, "like the pastrycook. Did you have to skin the rabbits yourself?" He could not bear the thought of that, he decided; it was a bloody, messy task; after they were married a servant should do it.

"No, Matthew, that's our man, skins them. Uncle Hurbert shot them and sent them down to us. This is going to be a raised pie — that is if you let me finish the pastry."

"I will be quiet, if you will let me watch," he promised, and sat back on a three-legged stool, from which vantage point his gaze never left her; watching the pretty figure, the slim waist, the busy arms and small, expert hands, rolling, spreading, pinching into shape, decorating with little balls of pastry at last brushed lightly with egg. Her eyelashes, generally considered a defect, he found enchanting.

"Pippa," he said, when the pies, three of them, were in the oven, "will you marry me?"

"You don't know me. We only met at the party. How can you want me to marry you, so soon?"

"I feel I have known you all my life. I want you to come and make me raised pies and marzipan sweets, and baste meat and braise fish, and make gravy, and any other damned thing you like. Or if you don't want to do any of it, it's all the same. Only say I can — how do they put it? — pay my addresses."

She had rinsed her hands from a stone jug, and was wiping them on her apron. A little smile, not unlike Jenny's, played about her face. "That would be a matter for Mama," she said, "or James."

"Your Mama is surrounded by suitors

41

of her own. Where do I find James?"

"Why, he is in his study, but he will not be pleased if you interrupt."

"Then he will have to be displeased, because I intend to do so."

Martin found James at his accounts. Marriage, and some money, had given the eldest remaining Volland son a sleek appearance; it was unlikely that he would be refused the position of vestryman now. On hearing what Martin had to say he at first stared incredulously, then put down his quill. "My sister is very young," was the first comment he had to make.

"I also am very young. We are both under twenty. It will be the best possible start in life."

James placed the tips of his fingers together. "You say 'will be'. I have not yet given my consent, nor has my mother. You must allow us time to consider the matter. You will realise, also, that my sister has no money."

"I have enough."

"What does your father say to it?" James knew who the Fieldings were; he made a point of knowing who everyone was, in the county and beyond. Martin smiled.

"My father is at the moment engrossed in talk with your mother. I doubt if Pippa and I have entered the conversation."

James was meantime thinking hard. It would be an excellent thing if one of the girls could be married with advantage; a pity that it must be Pippa, who so greatly added to the creature comforts of living! He knew that, unless some formidable obstacle presented itself, he himself would give his consent, and see to it that his mother gave hers. But such things must be taken slowly; this young man was too impetuous.

Anna herself was unwilling, for the same reason that James had fleetingly been so; tea would be dreadfully plain! Also, she resented the fact that one of her daughters was sought after in marriage; it brought the prospect of her own old age closer. How would Tillotson, how would Handley, regard the fact that she was a mother-in-law, possibly, very soon, a grandmother? It was different with James; men were always different. In any case he seldom seemed like her son.

In fact it was Uncle Hubert who sped everything on, after some weeks of almost daily visits from Martin Fielding and the sight of him and Pippa holding hands and following one another about Vollands: as Ocky said, there wasn't anything fit to eat nowadays. Uncle Hubert came striding into the room on a day when the assembled family were there, planted his considerable weight on a chair, and held forth. Since the defection of Eliza he had taken to heavy drinking, and his face was puffy, his eyes appearing narrowed in his head; they were presently fixed on James.

"What sort of damned fool are you? You get a good offer for the girl; mind, I don't say she isn't a good girl; best of the bunch, in my opinion, like my Jenny. But an offer's an offer, and the first you've had, maybe the last; what d'you want to be left with, a houseful of old maids? What are you waiting for? Get the banns to the parson, and have the wedding over before the winter; and, by God, I've given you enough money to buy the bride a gown. Where is she?

Where's Philippa? Damned if I know which of these wenches are which, they grow like leeks, a different size every time I come."

"I am here, Uncle Hubert," replied Pippa meekly. He stared at her, the narrowed eyes surveying her up and down.

"You'll do," he said. "Hear you're a cook. You want to marry this young man, or not?"

Pippa said she did. "Know what marriage means, eh?" said the martinet. "Look at Maud. There's some take to it worse than others. Y'mother never had any difficulty."

"Uncle Hubert, the girls," murmured Anna. In her corner Maud began to weep silently. She was accustomed to derogatory remarks about her appearance and state, but the sight of Papa had reminded her of home. If only she could go back! But marriage, everyone said, was for life. She looked forward to her own without enthusiasm. In all their time together, James had never addressed a single kind word to her, not even when he knew the baby was coming. And there might be more and more babies. It was in the family. How thankful she was to have Jenny, who was such a help! Now that Pippa was going away, she would be of more use than ever.

Philippa Volland and Martin Fielding were married on an autumn day of crisp air and blowing leaves. The bride, who had made her own cake, wore a becoming gown and flowered bonnet, and carried the bridegroom's bouquet into the decorated church: but the occasion was provided with its greatest glory by Hew and Buckland, who had obtained leave to attend the ceremony, and who lent the gleam of gold braid from their hussars' uniforms, their tall forms outshining that of James who gave the bride away, or Mark, who in a satin suit was the bridal attendant and had somehow been persuaded to behave. The young couple drove off at last to the noise of cheering, and Pippa's happy face was remembered for long afterwards by those who had been there on that day.

3

HEW stretched his long shapely legs, in their rough shooting gear, in front of him with Buckland beside him, similarly clad, on the sofa. The gorgeous uniforms had been left upstairs for the remainder of their leave, which by now was almost expired. Anna lay and watched her sons lazily; they were a handsome pair, but it would be necessary for them to marry heiresses. Fortunately there seemed no immediate necessity for this possibly difficult task; both young men were supremely happy in their chosen profession. She was so greatly occupied in studying Hew's dark head and Buckland's fair one that she did not become aware of what Hew was saying until he had in fact said half of it.

" — and so, Mama, we both decided to apply for service in Afghanistan. The Ameer has asked for aid in maintaining Peshawar, and although Lord Auckland has refused meantime, he cannot continue in such a way, for the honour of England. War will certainly come, and why should we moulder in barracks? A good many of the fellows feel as we do, and have asked to go out. They say that more than twenty thousand will in fact go."

"My dear boy, I do not know what an Ameer is, and I am not even certain that I could find the place you mention on Mark's schoolroom globe. It seems to me that it is foolish to risk your lives without need; England is not at war, and has not been since the time of Bonaparte, when you could have fought nearer home."

"War is our trade, Mama," put in Buckland unexpectedly. Anna shuddered.

"Do not, I beg of you, use that word; it is so very vulgar."

"Maybe; but it is the truth."

"Where is this Peshawar?" demanded Anna, showing that she had paid more heed than had been apparent. Hew assured her that it was the gateway to India; even Anna had heard of India; that the Persians on the one hand and the Sikhs on the other were trying to gain control, and an English commander named Pottinger had made a gallant defence at a place called Herat. "We shall go out under Sir John Keane, and hope to have some news to write to you soon," said Hew gaily. The prospect of war had lifted away his customary sternness of countenance and he looked like a boy again. Anna felt a sudden tug at her heart. Was she to lose all her sons? Harry was long gone; James was no comfort; Mark was too young. She moved restlessly on her cushions. They had told her Pippa was having a great success among the Fieldings' neighbours; she and Martin were asked everywhere. For oneself, it was dull with no one to see and nothing to eat worth mentioning; Jenny did her best, helped out by one or other of the Volland bastards Uncle Hubert sent down, then recalled as if he could not, after all, bear to lose them.

As though he had known what she was thinking Hew said, with a wink, "Guess who is living down at the men's quarters with her soldier? Eliza, and from the look of her the same thing is about to happen as happened so often with Uncle Hubert."

"Do not tell him," said Anna. At that moment Jenny, followed by Mark and the eldest bastard George, came in with the tea: the young girl had contrived to make some biscuits. "They are not like Pippa's, I fear," she said timidly when Hew told her how good they were, and asked for another. Jenny was not permitted to stay for tea. Her position was something between that of a servant and an unpaid companion to Maud, who by now had to wear a shawl to hide her figure, and had not come down. Jenny gave a little bob and was about to depart, when Hew put his arm about her and fed her a biscuit.

"Why shouldn't you have one, as you made them?" he said. He watched her go with regret; she was a pretty little thing, was Jenny. He himself was no hand with a pen, or he would write to her from Peshawar.

It was Buckland who wrote; Buckland who seemed to break, with a quill and ink, the silence which had always encompassed him. He wrote, from places so far away that they were beyond the imagination of those who received news of them, from Kandahar and Ghazni and Kabul; telling of the high snows in the Hindu Kush, the

Wind of a Hundred and Twenty Days that blew every year; the rubies and lapis-lazuli that lay waiting to be picked up by anyone passing; the sheep with fat stored in their tails; the fanatical people who lived on grapes and melons gathered in the double harvest of Afghanistan. "I am sending you, Mama, a rug made from sheep's wool and embroidered by the Barakzai tribesmen," he wrote. The rug arrived, covered in barbaric colours, and Anna put it in her own room, because it made all the other furnishings in the drawing-room seem faded by comparison. She was proud of having two sons at the war, especially as word came that Hew had been promoted to captain.

Then there came other word. Buckland would never write to them again. He had been killed by a Pathan spear in the Badakhshan passes.

"Permit me to look after you, my dear. You cannot stay here alone and grieving."

Squire Fielding had taken both Anna's hands in his, and pressed his suit as, by now, he had pressed it on many occasions since Pippa's wedding; and Anna tried as always to find a way of refusal which would neither hurt him nor remove him from her list of admirers. It was true that she grieved for Buckland: but it was a grief that concerned herself, and she knew it; never more to see his fair, shaggy head bent over a gun he was cleaning, or his big hands clutching a brace of game for her supper. It was one less in the family, as Harry's death had been, and her husband's. She thought of a way of silencing Fielding, cast up her eyes to Henry's miniature on the wall, and sighed.

"I could never be unfaithful to his memory," she said. "I was everything to him; I could never marry again."

"Of course you were everything to him; would be to any man," concurred the Squire gruffly. "Martin's wife is everything to *him*. I hardly see the boy now, he and Pippa are so constantly together; happy as sandboys, both of 'em. What the devil is a sandboy? And of course the comin' child pleases them greatly. I hope you will be with her then."

Anna retrieved one of her hands and

put a finger to her lips; Juley was in the room, and it was not proper to mention a coming child in a young girl's presence; although, come to think of it, Maud's hugeness increased daily and visibly and the birth was almost due. Juley must be without eyes if she had noticed nothing.

Juley's eyes were in fact kept lowered; later she would imitate the Squire's courtship to Ocky, but meantime she got on with the task of crochet Christian had left her: the foot-blankets were beginning to be called afghans. Christian herself was up at Hubertshall, visiting Ellen, with whom she had struck up a friendship. Juley could not think why; Maud's sister was a sharp, formidable woman, in addition to being plain like her sister. No doubt she was glad of company.

"Well, I'll take my leave," said the Squire at last, and did so. Once on his feet, he gazed down with longing at Anna. "Remember that if you should change your mind, I am at your service."

"My dear, dear friend, I will remember." She stretched out a hand; he kissed it gallantly, and went. Once he had gone Anna turned to Juley.

"Bring me a glass of negus, child, pray do. Such a visit makes me thirsty."

Maud Volland opened her mouth and yelled. The wing which she and James occupied was not large, and the sound would travel down to the main part of the house; but the labour was well begun and Maud was past caring. The bed was large, and by it sat Edith, ill at ease and with her hands clenched in her lap; and, with her from Hubertshall, one of the older women servants, who in her time had often acted as midwife to Eliza. Maud, in other words, might have been at home: her husband had looked in at the beginning to wish her easy pains and to tell her to make it a boy. Now that he was beginning to be successful in his financial ventures he was most anxious for a son to succeed him. Maud knew that her failure as a wife — her plainness, her inept ways, the fact that she had not brought a dowry in the usual sense — would be overlooked, if not forgiven, once she became the mother of an heir to Vollands. But now there was nothing but pain, this recurrent tearing agony; and so Maud yelled.

It went on all day, and from time to time the woman would come with a damp cloth to wipe the sweat from her face, tidy the pillows and try to make her comfortable; but she would never be comfortable again, she was convinced. Whatever was forcing its way down within her was large and determined; there was nothing she could do but scream; bear down, the woman kept saying, bear down, but it wasn't easy. Why did women have to suffer so? It was the punishment of Eve, James would have replied smugly; Maud could almost hear him say it, not that she had ever asked him such a question, for they had too little to say to one another for it to arise: But she was certain he would mention Eve, and punishment.

She yelled. It was the worst pain yet.

The waters had burst yesterday. She had been walking cautiously along the pebbled paths with Jenny, and it had happened, wetting and soiling her skirts. How glad she would be of Jenny's presence now! But the girl was not permitted to come up, although she must have assisted at many of her own mother's confinements.

Mrs Anna was suddenly prudish about such matters, treating Jenny like a daughter of her own, then at other times like a servant. Once the boy was born — God grant that it be a boy — she, Maud, must exert her authority a little; after all, she was the mistress of the house, though nobody would think it, the way things were run here.

Aaaaagh. Aaaaagh.

"Bear down, love. Bear down, and it'll come. It won't be long now. Bear down."

The shadows were lengthening outside; it must be getting towards evening. How long had she lain here, crying out, bearing down? A long time. James would be in his study. He wouldn't care if she died, as long as he had his son. He had never cared for her. It would have been better if he had taken Ellen. Ellen would have given as good as she got with her sharp tongue. She, Maud, was witless; never thought of an answer until it was too late.

Aaaaaagh. Ah — ah — ah — a sudden intolerable torment, then cessation of pain. The tears ran out of her eyes and streamed down on to the pillows.

"The head's come," said the woman.

"Mother — mother — "

"Yes, I am here," said Edith, the step-mother, ill at ease among the paraphernalia of birth. She herself had only had Ellen, and was glad of it.

"Here it is now," said the servant, and twisted the child's body out. Maud fell back flaccid on the pillows. She could take no interest in her child. She thanked God it was over. Please God, there would be no more.

Word was sent downstairs to James that he had a daughter. Presently he came up to the room, lips tight in anger. He did not look at the large lusty infant lying in its wrappings, but briefly at his wife, as though she had been an investment that had plummeted and lost money.

"It is all to be done again," he said coldly. Then he turned and went out.

In the following year Maud transgressed once more, and gave birth to a second girl. By that time the first, Anna Belinda, was charging about on her hobby-horse, being precocious as well as large. She was an enormous child with winning ways and a head of flaxen curls. By then the household at Vollands was plunged in sorrow for more than the death of Buckland. Pippa, who had been so happy in her marriage, for whom everything presaged good fortune, had died in childbirth. The news was brought by a red-eyed Squire, who said his son was inconsolable; if the baby had lived it would at least have been something, but they had lost both mother and child.

"I can hardly bear to walk through the house, and see the things she left, her little shapes for making pastries, and patty-pans and the like. I've told the servants to put 'em all away; they're in tears, they loved her. The whole county mourns her, I can tell you, and her only a bride. Why should she be taken and some left nobody cares for? I ask you, why?"

"What will Martin do?" asked Anna, to get him away from his own grief. The Squire looked at her directly.

"He has already said to me that he cannot bear Clarefountains alone, and begs me to allow him to go to sea, as

58

he always wanted to do," he said. "How can I refuse him? It will give the boy new places to visit, other company, hope for the future, an occupation. I told him he could go. After the funeral, he will make for Portsmouth."

"And you?" God forbid that he should ask her to marry him today, she thought; to refuse him would be unkind, and he was in sadness enough.

But he looked at her in silence. "I shall sell Clarefountains," he said, "and take myself off, possibly to some watering-place. Our house has been in Fielding hands ever since James I came down from Scotland. But now there's nobody to inherit; it may as well go to younger folk, with children of their own."

Anna's thoughts flickered briefly towards Christian, seated demurely in her chair; could the Squire not make a marriage with her? But Christian was cold, bookish; she would be no comfort to a man who had loved Pippa. Anna said nothing, and let the Squire go.

In fact he, after Martin's departure and the sale of the house, took himself to the new resort still building at Bournemouth.

After a year or two there he met a sprightly widow with a consuming interest in cards. Over games of cribbage or the new bézique they discovered companionship, then friendship; and that was enough. The second Mrs Fielding put an end to his loneliness; their lives were passed agreeably together, for a surprising term of years, and when one died the other was not long following. Martin never married again; he became a much respected and loved naval officer, and went down at last fighting gallantly in the Dardanelles, on the way to protect Constantinople from the Russians.

4

THE last slate had been laid in place on the roof of Hubertshall, and the gilded ship spun merrily in the wind. Old Hubert Volland, a few days away from his seventy-first birthday, strode up and down before the front of the house, looking up, seeing that everything was as it should be, as he had planned it from the first. Long after he was dead this house would stay, up on the hill where he had foreseen it, had month after month and year after year worked out every tower and hall and wing. It was built of red stone, which had had to be brought from a distance; this pleased Hubert; nobody else had a house that colour, no one in the county or beyond. The county itself, for this very reason, should come and admire his house: he would have a shooting-party. He went over in his head the names of those who should be invited. Edith would be incapable of instructing the cooks; he would do it himself, and roasted oxen, roasted sheep, should not be lacking, any more than the flow of wine. The tenants should have a bonfire; everything should be done as it ought to be, as it had been done from old times. There would be a dance in the barn for the ordinary folk, and the rest, his invited guests, should regale themselves inside the house after a day with the guns. The guns! The cock pheasants would have to be flushed out, the partridges driven in. A pity young Hew and Buckland hadn't been here; they would have helped him prepare the coverts. His bastard boys would have to do: and Jenny should come. Little Jenny, the best of the bunch, should oversee the cooks; she'd learned enough down at Anna's.

He sent out his invitations, regretting that, owing to mourning for Pippa, Squire Fielding and his son could not come; both were good shots. There was one name on his list which gave him pleasure, an acquaintance he had made haphazardly; the Earl of Munster, the King's eldest illegitimate son. Munster was a moody devil, they said he didn't get on with his wife, but he enjoyed a shoot. Word came back that he had accepted, and would come.

The tenants' bonfire blazed orange against the night, and whole families from the cottages feasted on ox roasted whole, with the dripping falling dangerously into the fire. There was dancing and leaping back and forth into the well-fed flames; whoever came through unscathed would be married within the year. Young Jenny took time off from her task of seeing to the cooks, who were doing well enough on their own, and stood nearby the fire, her cheeks bright. Someone shouted, "Jenny! Jenny! Jump through the fire and get yourself a man!" then everyone laughed, because Jenny was so pretty there would be no difficulty about that. She laughed, blushed and shook her corn-gold head; she would not jump through the flames.

Upstairs, in the house, Hubert and the Earl of Munster were examining a pistol George IV had given the latter. "He was kind enough," said Munster. "They talked against him a good deal." He took up the pistol to show off its silver chasings, and Hubert bent close to see. There was an explosion; the pistol had gone off unexpectedly. Hubert clapped a hand to his eye. Presently the blood ran down, thick and crimson.

They sent for doctors, but there was nothing they could do; the bullet had entered the front of the brain, and it was only a matter of time till death. Hubert lay, with one side of his head bandaged, in bed, and bade farewell to all his family; the shooting-party had dispersed. Close against his pillow sat Jenny, the tears running down her face; he held tight to her hand, saying again and again what he had so often said, that she was the best of them all. The sound eye slewed about to look at her.

"You'll make some man happy, as you made me," Hubert said. "Guard yourself; don't take the first comer."

He died at sunset. James was with others in the room; he had come up in the carriage. Christian would stay with Ellen. Edith had burst into loud sobs, inexplicably because she had had no feeling for the dead man nor he for her. The vast body was covered by a sheet, and the disfigured face. Everyone left the death-chamber except Jenny, who remained sobbing by the bed.

"Come away," said a voice. "Come with me."

It was James. He picked her up and, carrying her, took her down to the carriage. He placed her in it and gave the driver a wink. She was still sobbing and crying, almost swooning; she hardly seemed to know where she was, or with whom.

"Papa! Papa! Oh, dear Papa!"

The horses started up. There was a second way they could take, which made a loop, wooded by trees, on the way back to Vollands. The driver made no haste, and to the gentle clip-clop of the hooves James let his hands explore Jenny's young body, at first pretending to comfort her. She wept on, taking no heed. Presently James slid his hands up her skirts, rucking them above her knees; and made no more delay. She cried out then, but it was too late; he found her desirable, a welcome relief from Maud's scraggy frame. To the jogging of the horses he accomplished his will; if she cried, if she struggled, nobody heard except the driver, who took no heed. Mr Volland paid him, not the wench; his task was to see and know nothing, and attend to the horses.

The road was long, the pace slow. James had plenty of time to take his pleasure. He had had his eye on Jenny for a long time. Now the old man was dead, it was safe. There would be other opportunities. With Vollands at last in sight he pulled her skirts down tidily, and fastened his trousers. The tears were still running down Jenny's face; he was not disturbed: they would think it was for her father.

"I'll have a baby," she wailed. She had seen enough of them born to her mother, and knew how they came. James laughed.

"Trust me not to let you," he told her. He had in fact been cautious.

She clutched her hands against her breast in shame. How would she face Mrs Anna? And poor, poor Papa, whom she had loved dearly, and who was dead, had said to her only today, as he was dying, "Guard yourself; don't take the first comer." And she had, but without meaning to; almost without knowing what had happened.

She felt James lift her down from the carriage, and made her way into the house. Her red eyes were to be expected; nobody asked any questions. Jenny went upstairs to her room, and once there howled aloud.

Uncle Hubert's will, made after Eliza's desertion, was read following the funeral. The fact that it was Munster who had caused the accident was enough to hush things up, and the verdict of death by misadventure was not called in question. It was in fact considered a fitting end for one who had lived in as eccentric a manner as the deceased. His bequests, however, were sane enough. Everything, practically speaking, was left to James; Vollands and Hubertshall, the farms and cottages, the investments and securities, with two provisos; one being that Edith and Ellen be allowed to live on at Hubertshall with the payment of a small allowance, and the other that the tenants' cottages and farms should be kept in good repair. Of the bastards, even Jenny, there was no mention. It was as though the absconding of Eliza had forfeited any rights her children might have held in their father's remembrance.

After the will had been read, and everybody had returned home, Christian asked James to spare her a few moments of his time. This surprised him; he and his eldest sister had little in common, and he supposed her to be entirely taken up with Anna, her books, and her letters to Rugby. He rose courteously, and bade her be seated; but Christian declined.

"Ellen and I have a plan, if you will allow it, for Hubertshall," she said. "We worked it out long ago, when Uncle Hubert was still alive. As you will know, it is far too large to be used as an ordinary house. We thought of making it into a girls' school."

"That would cost a great deal in alterations; and how would you pay the teachers you employ?" His prudent nature put difficulties in the way of most things; at the same time, his mind was turning over the project. He had in fact been wondering what in the world to do with Hubertshall. Ellen would make an admirable headmistress, with Christian to support her, all of the latter's knowledge being no doubt of great benefit; she had read all her life, and by now must know more than most governesses put together. He looked at her; a handsome woman, presentable to parents; there was one objection.

"What about Mama? Who is to look after her?"

"There are Juley and Octavia; they can surely take it in turn to do so."

"And if they marry?"

"That is in the future," said Christian primly. "In fact Mama needs very little looking after. I have thought over this for a considerable time, and have had excellent advice on the matter from Dr Arnold."

"Will you flog your pupils as he flogs his?" asked James with unaccustomed humour. Christian did not echo it, or smile.

"There will be appropriate punishment; not perhaps as harsh as that for boys. We hoped that expensive fees might be obtained, which would assure careful supervision of the girls."

"It will certainly not be worth undertaking for cheap ones. I assume that influence can be brought to bear to ensure the enrolment of daughters of the best families?"

"Daughters of rich families will do very well," said Christian, lightening in her turn. "It is no longer impossible for the children of tradesmen to associate with those of the nobility, if there is enough money. We would endeavour to teach manners and deportment to each girl, irrespective of whence she came."

"I will think it over," James promised: and Christian departed knowing that she had, almost certainly, won.

Jenny slept in an attic room with an iron-framed bed, a jug and ewer on a stand, and underneath a chamber-pot which she emptied and rinsed daily. She knew that she was fortunate to have a room of her own; it was due to the fact that there were so few servants at Vollands. Her mother Eliza had taught her to be clean, and every night she washed herself in cold water brought up from the well, then pulled on her flannel nightgown and after brushing out her hair, got into bed. In summer the room, which was under the roof, was too hot, in winter bitterly cold; but it was what everyone had to put up with.

She had not yet blown out her candle when the latch of the door tilted up, and James entered the room noiselessly. Jenny felt her heart pounding: she had been almost certain that he would come, after what happened on the road. In fact, she was bewildered and frightened; Mr James was master of everything, and could turn her out of the house with nowhere to go, if she didn't let him do what he wanted. There was no Papa now to whom to run. There was nothing to do but stay here, and submit.

She submitted. When he had done again as he would the bed began to rock with his repeated thrustings, and Jenny was afraid they would hear it downstairs. She cried out something of the kind, and he laughed, setting his mouth hard against hers.

"Always afraid, aren't you, my Jenny? You be a good girl, and do as I say, and you won't be sorry." And he went on for a good while, and had her panting, and then he got off her and out of her bed, kissed her, and went away. She lay where he had left her and felt the awakened blood pound in her body: as long as there wasn't a baby, and he had promised there wouldn't be, she supposed she was getting used to it.

He came to her most nights after that, and it seemed to Jenny that she must look different, that they would notice the difference somehow by day; but no one said anything. At the same time she wondered why he came upstairs to her in the cold; now that Mrs Maud was midway through her third pregnancy she slept alone in the back bedroom, and Mr James in the master room, which was warm and comfortable. But he never invited Jenny down there, and in his cautious way never made it obvious, when the others were present, that there was anything special about her. Mrs Maud relied on her, as always, for all manner of things, fetching and carrying, or simply comfort. She was very much afraid of this coming birth, and had turned into a whining spiritless creature, with no pleasure in the two little girls, Anna Belinda and Maudie. It was Jenny who played with them, saw to it that they ate their food, mended their clothes when they tore them, and took them out in the fine weather, Anna Belinda walking on her big-boned legs and Maudie still in a baby-carriage. Jenny pushed it, and dangled toys in front of Maudie's face; she was not a pretty baby, neither of them were. Perhaps when the boy came at last their father would take some notice of all his children. Their father; her possessor. The Mr James who came to her at nights was no different, after all, from the self-important personage who sat at a desk doing accounts all day and went to vestry meetings now that he had been elected. He was still important to himself when in her bed.

Alterations had been going on at Hubertshall in preparation for the opening of the new school in the following spring; the sounds of hammering disturbed Edith, who seldom ventured forth from her rooms. Ellen on the other hand was everywhere, having at last found a vocation, a meaning for her life. She had given up doing her hair in side-curls as was still the fashion, and had dragged it back into a handsome bun at the back of her head; she wore dark high-necked dresses, as though the girls were already in residence and able to watch and fear her; and she consulted Christian constantly. The carriage came more frequently up from Vollands than their own went down the hill; Christian had almost shed her old home, and Anna now was left in charge of the younger girls.

A great privilege was accorded to Ellen and Christian at this time. It was half-term, and Dr Arnold was able to spare the time to come over from Rugby to see and advise on the new school. He arrived, a short stocky man with thick, rumpled dark hair and clergyman's bands, full of brisk energy. He had with him his eldest son, Matthew, who said not a word except in Mark Volland's company; they were about the same age. Even then he followed his father constantly with his eyes; he evidently worshipped him.

"Too clever for me by half," muttered Mark afterwards. "If they're all like that, nobody else will win any prizes."

Dr Arnold, who was a believer in exercise, refused the use of the carriage, and strode up the hill to Hubertshall on foot in the same way as, when he had leisure, he would stride over the green places near his country house of Fox How in Westmorland, to seek out and pick wild flowers. Even here he bent now and again to collect bugle, eyebright, vetch and cinquefoil, giving them into Matthew's keeping to hold in his small hot fists. Ocky, who was with them, and had no fear of persons, questioned this.

"They'll only die," she said. "Why not leave them growing?"

The famous headmaster's scholarly brow bent itself towards her kindly. "We all of us have only a little moment to live, my dear," he told her. Ocky stared at him; for herself, she hoped to live rather longer.

They inspected the school, and Dr Arnold made several suggestions, such as that the governesses should have rooms of their own, not mere cubicles railed off from the dormitories. "It will cost more," said Ellen. "James may complain." James was having to be consulted about every least improvement; he could be astonishingly mean.

"Tell your brother that that particular outlay will repay him. If a teacher has privacy it gives room and time for thought, and the thought is expended later on the pupils. You should also advertise very early in the gazettes, even before everything is ready, for your April start."

They told James all of it later, and because Dr Arnold had said it it was allowed. The Doctor was staying at Vollands over the weekend, and accompanied the family to church, with Matthew by him. James had had the immense gratification, lately, of being made a vestryman after all. He stood in the side aisle, watching his mother, still beautiful, shown to her place, followed by Maud, full of her pregnancy (Mrs Arnold, being as usual in the same state, had been unable to accompany her husband), the young sisters, and, in the row behind, the servants and Jenny, in charge of his own two children. James felt lust rise whenever he looked at Jenny; she wore, as was suitable, a plain dark gown and bonnet, with her bright hair smooth below the brim. The bodice of the gown was low-cut, revealing an expanse of white neck and indicating her bosom, which was no longer that of a child; his handling had ripened it. Tonight, he thought, when he went to her, he would strip her naked, as it was summer. Little by little he was debauching her; by now, he could make her moan with pleasure once he had entered her, and stayed within her long enough; but one had to be prudent. Jenny would make an excellent mother, but he had to remember that it was his business to ensure that she did not become one. His position in the county, which he was slowly building up since Uncle Hubert's inheritance had fallen to him, would suffer if it were known he had a mistress, let alone a child by her.

He turned his eyes away now, in order not to be caught watching her from his seat, which he had taken. The clergyman, Dr Band, had already come in and the service was proceeding.

Afterwards it would be gratifying to make him known to the famous Dr Arnold of Rugby, one's guest. He would, James thought with irritation, have been asked to dinner to meet the headmaster, had it not been for the possibility, mentioned by the physician, of Maud's going into early labour on this occasion. Maud was an inconvenience in every possible way except one: perhaps, this time, she would justify herself.

5

THE good Dr Arnold and his son Matthew took themselves off, to the farewells of the assembled family. Christian particularly was in a state of trance; she had actually had her idol close to her for two days and nights, and he had made her an affectionate speech on parting and wished her well in her venture! For it was *her* venture; Ellen would never have thought of it for herself, although Ellen proved to have surprisingly advanced ideas now that there was a prospect of carrying them out.

Anna was languid; she had failed to arouse any interest in Dr Arnold, and that meant that he did not interest her either. When Christian rhapsodised about his improvements at Rugby, the ways in which he had turned it from a chaotic assembly to an oncoming, positive school, Anna gave her famous yawn behind a hand and bade her daughter be silent.

"We have heard quite enough of

schools," she said. "From what I hear, his wife has a child each year, so his mind cannot be entirely centred on his schoolbooks and his flogging."

"Mama, you should be more particular in what you say," replied Christian, flushing; she had taken on authority since the prospect of her school neared completion. There was a guffaw from the foot of Anna's chaise-longue; from Bartholomew Tillotson, who had ridden in that day, and who had just been in time to encounter Dr Arnold as the latter departed. Juley, who was present, writhed with laughter; she was growing fast into an attractive young lady, and Tillotson's eye was no longer entirely fixed on Anna. He had, in fact, debated with himself more than once how it would be possible to make the closer acquaintance of Miss Juley; with her mother in the room it was impossible to give the daughter much attention, and Mr Tillotson found increasingly that he wanted to. As he flattered Anna, he would look from time to time towards the young girl, who had the grace of a nymph, and no self-conscious manners such as were instilled into young ladies nowadays. Tillotson thought that he would like to instruct Juley in the arts of living, concerning most of which he knew a little; but how to broach the matter to her Mama? Anna Volland would resent the transference of attention from herself to her daughter.

If he had known, Anna had noticed everything; and did not resent it at all. She was beginning to find Tillotson wearisome with his old-maidish ways: Handley was in attendance on his mother, who was ill; and it would be restful to be alone, and to read Hew's laconic accounts, which arrived regularly, of the Afghan war.

James ascended the stairs noiselessly that summer night, aware that he had no protection from darkness. There was, on the other hand, no need of a candle; he could make his way unaided to Jenny's door by now. He went in, as usual, without knocking, and found her half undressed. He watched her gown fall about her, and saw her, hesitantly, pull her chemise up over her head. When she reached for her nightgown he said. "Leave it. Stay as you are."

She stood naked, having folded her clothes; she felt her knees tremble. It was always worse when he took her without a gown. He made her lie down on the bed, and she obeyed; he took off his own clothes swiftly, and presently came and lay with her, at the same time running his hands over the peach-bloom flesh. "Jenny, Jenny," he murmured, and she could take leisure to think how there was seldom any speech between them; in fact they had nothing to say to one another.

He was fondling her breasts, and kissing them. She was aware of a shiver throughout her body; his handling, his using of her, his taking her, made it happen. Again the bed began to creak, and she moved beneath him restlessly, certain she heard someone coming up the stairs. His hands had left her breasts by now and as usual closed on her upper arms; these were bruised with his pitiless gripping of them night after night. It didn't show by day, beneath her gown.

He was well within her now, prolonging his enjoyment carefully as always. She took no part in the pleasure, except for what came despite James Volland; the response, the late hot beating of the blood, the delicious enchantment flowing at last from the womb. Jenny began to babble, and at that moment the door opened and into the room walked Maud.

"I thought Anna Belinda had a rash this evening, and I was going to ask you, Jenny, to go down and — "

Her mouth dropped open, revealing the discoloured teeth. Her swollen body was like a bulwark, advancing despite itself or her. Then she screamed aloud, seized Jenny's hair, and pulled and pulled at it, screaming still. Jenny began to cry. James left the bed, stood up, found his shirt, held it in front of him, and said to his wife, "Go back to your room. Go back at once. You should not be here."

"*I* should not be here? *I* should not be? You are my husband, and *she* — You little trollop! Pretending you were helping me! Out you go tomorrow!"

The tears were rolling down her uncomely face; she had let go of Jenny's hair, and stood there crying helplessly. James was dressing himself with what dignity he could contrive. When he had done so he turned to his wife.

"You will leave Jenny alone. If you ever mention one word of this occurrence to anyone, I will have you confined as insane. Remember it. Now go downstairs, as I told you; and on no account come up here again."

He turned her by the shoulders, and propelled her out of the room. He had neither said a word to Jenny nor done anything to comfort her. Left alone, she crept shivering under the covers despite the summer night, and wondered if Mrs Maud would indeed send her away, and if so where she would go. Certain things had happened to her she had not asked for; and now she was different, in a way she could not explain.

Maud sent nobody anywhere. She went into labour at four in the morning and, by noon, had miscarried of a dead boy. If James regarded this episode as a punishment for his own shortcomings he gave no sign of it; coldly, as usual, he blamed his wife. Thereafter he continued to visit Jenny's room, oblivious to her distress. As soon as Maud had recovered sufficiently he made it his business to ensure that she was, again, shortly made pregnant. This time it proved, once more, a girl; and a fourth daughter was born in the following year. By now, Maud was almost the insane creature James had threatened to have confined; terror had overcome her nights and days. He had no mercy on her; had he had his way she would have continued to give birth yearly for the rest of her breeding life. But, after the arrival of little Adela, there were, for whatever reason, no more children. When this became apparent, James took thought to himself; he must, by whatever means, obtain a son.

The new school at Hubertshall was declared officially open in April, when the countryside was looking its best, if not the grounds; there had hardly been time since the winter to do more than dig and prepare these. The parents who flocked to the opening day were assured that each pupil would be given her own little plot to cultivate, and that there would be a prize at the end of the year for the best garden.

Meantime, among the items required to be brought in hair trunks were a trowel, a fork, and gardening gloves. This was agreed to be significant of the advanced nature of projected education at the new school, which as well as the customary subjects would also teach simple cookery and accounts. It was true that girls commonly entered the state of marriage ill-prepared, some not even knowing how to boil an egg or make tea; and this state of affairs would at least be ameliorated by a sojourn at Hubertshall. Ellen and Christian, moving about among their guests, gave full credit to Dr Arnold, who had come today to declare the school open, for every one of the above suggestions: and any doubt the more conservative parents might have had was soon dispelled by the confident speech the great headmaster made, filling everyone, in the way he had, with certainty that all was for the best. In fact, several brothers of girls enrolled at Hubertshall were sent to Rugby as a result of this personal meeting with the Doctor, who was made known to the parents over tea. Altogether it was a most auspicious beginning; the sun shone, conveying clear light through the sparkling windows; the dormitories were swept and dusted, the pinewood desks in the classrooms polished till they gleamed; and, prominently displayed, was the set of volumes of Thucydides which Dr Arnold had himself edited and which he had brought with him today to give as an opening tribute to Christian, signed by his own hand.

Christian's younger sisters were less well entertained; nobody took any notice of them. Octavia sat at a tea-table, observing the people who passed; Juley wandered off. She went into the house, less out of curiosity concerning the school than out of affection for the memory of old Uncle Hubert, who had been kind to her now and again. She was gazing at an altered wall with a door put into it when she heard a man's voice speak.

"May I direct you anywhere? I think that perhaps you are lost. It is a large building."

She turned, and beheld a fairly young man, not tall, with receding hair and a pale, pleasant face. Ocky would have bristled at being addressed by a stranger, but Juley smiled. "I knew this house before it was a school," she said. "It was built by my uncle; my great-uncle, that is."

"Was his name Hubert Volland? I think I have heard of him."

"Everybody here has heard of him. He was like a great naughty boy."

He laughed, showing white teeth. "Permit me to introduce myself," he said. "I am Thomas Byrne, and I hope to start the new term here as drawing-master."

"I am Julia Volland. Shall you like teaching silly girls?"

He grimaced a little. "One has to earn a living. Will you walk about the grounds with me a little, Miss Julia? I am sure you are not a silly girl; and it will be a pleasant interlude for me to remember when I have, as you say, to start teaching them."

She laid her hand on his arm, and they went outside and walked about, talking of almost everything, for what seemed a short time, but was in fact almost an hour.

"It was improper for you to go off like that, with a stranger," Octavia said. "I really think that I should report to Mama how you behaved."

"Mama will not care. She will be glad that I found a personable young man to talk with."

"He is only the drawing-master. I asked Lady Yester, who came to speak to me. I am sure she thought it was very singular that you were not there."

"You are turning into a little prig, Ocky," said Julia. They did not speak again till it was time to go home.

James Volland had stood about among the crowd, acknowledging acquaintance here and there. He saw Juley pass by on her swain's arm, but it did not trouble him; he thought only of himself, and was agreeably conscious that he was spoken of not only as the owner of the school, but as a rising figure both in the county and the City, where he had to go now and again to see to his investments, to visit his tailor, and to make certain contacts which would ensure his future. His position as a vestryman, once so avidly desired, now seemed very small beer indeed; to be invited to become a Justice of the Peace, even a Member of Parliament, were not beyond the bounds of possibility for an ambitious, and cautious, young man. His behaviour remained, accordingly, prudent. Jenny was not present, although her brothers and sisters were, carrying teapots and cake-plates, removing them when they were finished with, and washing them up behind the scenes. It had been a question of whether or not the bastard Volland family should be allowed to remain at Hubertshall for the sake of the school's reputation; but, as Ellen rightly said, they knew the house, and their own place, and would be unlikely in any case to say who they were; also, it did away with the need for hired servants, who might be unreliable. So George, the eldest son, and the rest passed back and forth, unacknowledged by James or anybody else; they would in fact remain in their father's house till they were old men and women, having known no other home.

Jenny, left in charge of the four tow-headed little girls, was unaware of any difference in her day. She acted as nursemaid to them as usual, sitting with them in the nursery, taking meals with them, seeing that the baby was fed on its pap; dealing with Anna Belinda, who was like a large young monkey, everywhere at a time, asking questions Jenny did not know how to answer. Once a day their mother looked in, ignoring Jenny; stared at the children, never spoke to them, and took herself off; there was a feeling of relief when she had gone. Now and again, also, Mrs Anna came; and that was different. She would sit in a chair and draw the children to her, and tell them wonderful stories of fairies and dragons, which the baby could not of course understand: and Jenny was certain that Mrs Anna was entertaining herself as much as the children. Sometimes a young man or two would come with her, and toss up Adela or Beatrice or Maudie, but never Anna Belinda, who was much too large, in their arms. Then the laughing party would go back downstairs, leaving Jenny to calm the excited children and try to interest them in their few toys.

James never visited the nursery; his

children did not know him. Accordingly, when he stood in the doorway on the evening of the school opening, Anna Belinda opened her mouth and screamed; some of the others began to cry. "Be silent," said James. He took Jenny by the forearm and led her to the window-embrasure. "I have to give you certain instructions," he told her. "If those children cannot be quiet they must be whipped till they are. Listen to me, if you can hear me above the noise." He looked round in irritation, still thumbing the flesh of Jenny's forearm. "I want you," he said slowly, "to come downstairs to me in future, to the master bedroom."

He passed his tongue over his lips. She heard him without pleasure; she had once wondered why he didn't ask her down there, and had rightly guessed that it was in case anyone found out that he was coming to her, or she to him. She knew enough now to be aware of his cold ambition, his caution lest anyone suspect that he repeatedly used her body. She heard him explaining about the master room, as if it were something he was trying to sell her.

"It is a feather mattress, very deep and comfortable. You will never have slept in such a bed. I want you to wait until everyone is asleep, then come; not earlier than eleven o'clock, and you must be gone again by morning. You will undress in the room; do not bring your nightgown with you." The thumb caressed her arm continually; his eyes surveyed her as though she were already naked. She thought of the exhausting days, spent in looking after his children; and now the nights, naked and deep in the feather mattress beneath him for hours, then back to her own cold room. It wasn't so bad at this time of year, but —

"You will come," he told her, and it was not a query but a command. He left her to deal with the screaming little girls, and went out.

She had indeed never lain on such a mattress. Her light weight sank into it, the deep thickness of feathers almost enclosing her, warming her after the cold groping journey downstairs. Almost, for instants, she gave herself to the unknown comfort, forgetting that Mr James was undressing to come to her; then he came. For the first time, and this shocked her, he also was naked. She felt his lean cool flesh against her own, and would have recoiled; but there was no escape in this yielding bed. She closed her eyes in the dark; that way, he seemed further off.

He was using her differently tonight; making no haste to lie with her, but caressing her with his hands all over, touching places that made her feel ashamed; thumbing, smoothing, exploring, so that it seemed that there was no part of her body he had not roused to fire. Jenny felt, in the dark, her cheeks grow crimson; why was he like this? It was as though he were preparing her for something; but what?

She soon knew. When he entered her, he did not withdraw early, as was his custom, and come again. He lay with her till at last she felt the warm outpouring of semen flood her. She cried out and sobbed, struggled and tried to free herself, as on that first day of all in the carriage; but could not.

"You promised there wouldn't be a baby," she wept. She could remember the anguished cries in labour of Maud, of her own mother. She didn't mind babies, but she didn't want his. She heard him laugh quietly.

"I have decided that there shall be one, Jenny," he told her. "It will be born very privately. I want a son. If you give me one, I will adopt him. He will inherit all I have. That is a fine prospect for you, is it not?"

She did not reply. He continued to enjoy her, while the tears ran down her cheeks. He was aware of pleasure well fulfilled, of the orgasm he had not formerly, out of caution, permitted himself with her; now, there should be others. It had seemed appropriate that his son should be begotten in the master bed, where Volland heirs had been conceived for generations. Jenny should come to him here night after night till it was certain. It was unfortunate that, in the midst of his keenest pleasure, he had to go in a few days to London, to an important meeting of shareholders, and had arranged to be away for some time on other business as well. But on return — perhaps even now — the matter should be resolved. He smiled in the darkness, feeling Jenny still trembling beneath him. She was a good little creature; he would soon accustom her to the new state of things. Meantime, to have her smooth warm nakedness here with him in the deep feather bed was pleasant; a pity he could not prolong the pleasure till the morning, but one's reputation was of the first importance.

Jenny crept miserably downstairs for four more nights before James meant to leave. Every night in the master bed was the same, except that, by now, he was lying ready in it, waiting for her. When she would try to draw the curtains on her side before taking off her clothes, he would tell her to leave them open; he liked to watch her undress: She could feel his pale eyes fastened on her while she undid buttons and tapes, removed shoes, garters, stockings, gown, chemise. At last, climbing unwillingly into the bed, she would feel him take her, and always at thought of a baby would weep silently. When James set his mouth against her lips and cheeks they were wet. By degrees he grew impatient with her.

"You should be proud to bear my son," he told her, and once upbraided her with being a bastard Volland. Nightly the ready seed would be forced into her; she grew more and more afraid that the baby had started.

On the last night he abandoned caution, and kept her with him all night till the light showed for early morning. She had to get up, huddle on her clothes, and prepare for another day; a day with the squalling children, a day with a cold visit from Mrs Maud, perhaps another from Mrs Anna: neither of them guessing that she came down here nightly. Tomorrow night, though, she could stay alone in her own bed. There would be a few days of freedom.

James left in his carriage on a Tuesday, and by Sunday Jenny made a discovery that filled her with relief. Her period had come. There wasn't any baby yet. If only she could go away somewhere! If only there was somebody she could tell! But there was no one. Mrs Anna, Mrs Maud, Miss Octavia — she wasn't sure about Miss Juley, but it wouldn't be proper — would all be against her, wouldn't listen or help. If Miss Pippa had lived it might have been different. But that was the way things were.

Something in fact happened now to alter Jenny's whole life. In the continued absence of James, Hew Volland arrived home from the army for a few days' leave. It was five years since they had seen him.

He had arrived early in the morning, before the family were out of bed. He stood waiting by the window, looking out at the March day. There was a brief frost silvering the ground, soon to be dispelled by the pale early sun, bringing warmth and hope to the growing shoots which were still partly underground. It was long since he had had leisure to stand and look out of a window at a garden. With the hazards of war, and the forever remembered sight of Buckland lying dead in his blood, Hew's face had grown hard and bitter. As a young man it had been that of a hawk; now it was an eagle's, the great nose and heavy-lidded eyes surveying the world with irony and lack of trust. He was lean and erect with riding and marching in the defiles of the half-known mountains; outside, his horse was being rubbed down by his batman, who had come with him and who would sleep in the stable quarters with the coachman. Hew expected his mother and sisters to come down soon; there was no haste: he had breakfasted on the journey.

But it was Jenny who came, soft-footed; Jenny, on her way to the nursery.

He turned at the light sound she made. She paused uncertainly, for an instant not knowing him; the dark-haired, vital boy who used to come lounging in from a day's shooting with Buckland had gone. There were threads of grey in this man's hair. At first his great height and presence filled her with fear, and then —

"Jenny! Little Jenny!"

He held out his arms; she was too shy to go into them, but instead gave him her hands, and he gripped them, and stood her away from him, looking at her. They looked in fact at one another; there was no need of words between them. Hew could not take his eyes from her, aware that though she had changed, she was still Jenny. She had put on flesh, if he had known, with lovemaking; her bosom was that of a goddess, her waist taut and trim, her unseen thighs rounded now as a courtesan's, her mouth grown full with kissing. But he only saw her as the woman promised by the girl he remembered well; the girl who had been in his mind even while he had taken Indian harlots as they all did, brown limbs and breasts only, never faces. This was the woman for him. "Jenny, Jenny." He could only say her name.

He recollected himself presently. "My mother and sisters will be down soon," he said. "When may I see you alone?" The dark bright eyes were suddenly wide open beneath their lids, surveying her. Jenny clung to his hands as if to a lifeline. Why could he not have come before?

"I am in the nursery all day," she said quietly. Hew frowned; he didn't want squalling brats to interrupt them. "When are you free?" he asked. "Quick, Jenny; I can hear them above stairs."

"Not till I put the children to bed. That will be at half past five. Then you will have your dinner." She could map out his day clearly, as if he had been a part of herself; she could think for him, already.

"I will meet you after dinner, then, on the terrace. Bring your cloak; it will be cold."

A step sounded on the stairs; it was Mrs Anna, freshly combed and dressed. "Hew! My dearest boy!"

The white hands reached out to engulf him. He went dutifully to kiss her. Jenny had fled. He was not interested in the others; he wished he had been free to follow her after all, despite the children. Tonight must come quickly. He only had leave for a short time, but it would be enough. He saw Juley and Octavia come down after their mother. Octavia was plump and pretty, still with her curly hair and rosy cheeks; Juley was graceful, but too thin. He kissed them all; and regretted that he had not kissed Jenny. He would make up for that tonight. The day would pass somehow.

Jenny was late, because Anna Belinda had been difficult to get to bed, and the others slow to sleep. She ran downstairs and across the room where she had met Hew in the morning, and out through the terrace door, and along to where he was waiting. He put his arm about her, and led her down the steps.

"Let us go somewhere away from here," he said. She let him take her by the ways they both knew; across the lawn, towards the coppice, within sound of the running stream where sometimes, in season, as a boy, he had used to fish. She said no word and no more did he; there was no need for anything but silence between them.

The coppice was dry; there had been no rain. There was the sound of the stream close by. He spread his cloak for her to sit on the ground and, once there, lay down with his head on her lap. "Jenny," he said again. "Jenny." She laughed.

"You can't say anything but my name."

"I have said it to myself more often than you know; in strange places, in cold mountains, in the teeming cities of India."

"Tell me about them." Her fingers were in his thick hair, caressing it. She was aware of supreme contentment. This was her man, and she'd known it in an instant, and so had he. Whatever he asked now, she would do. She listened, while his voice flowed on; but rather to the sound of it than to what he was saying.

"I saw my brother dead. He had been like the other half of me. After that I was alone. I did not care whether I lived or died, and that made me careless of what happened, and so I could accomplish more than most men. We toppled the Ameer from his place; I myself was with that party, and we took him to Calcutta, where bodies float thick in the river mud and the streets are thronged with naked beggars. His son Akbar Khan continued to fight us, and will do more harm yet. Our man, Shah Shuja, may not stay the course; who knows? Soon I must go back."

"Do not go." Her arms tightened about him. "Take me with you? Do not leave me here."

He turned so that he looked up at her face. "Why, we will be married, Jenny," he said. "Will you trust yourself to a soldier of fortune? It is all I am; but my heart you have, and you know it."

"And you have mine." Suddenly she

leant forward and set her lips on his. At the movement he began to tremble; he put his arms about her; she could feel the hard muscles beneath his uniform sleeves.

"Jenny." He had begun kissing her as she had never been kissed before; differently from James's dry precise kisses; hard, urgent, taking no denial. The question he asked was not put into other words than these; she knew what he wanted of her. She would give him her body, gladly, now; with a joy that had never come to her before. She laid her soft cheek against his hard one.

"Yes," she whispered. "Yes."

"You little whore."

It was much later. He had risen from her at last, having contemptuously slaked his need. He fastened his clothes and turned away, unwilling to recall her pale face as she lay there dishevelled in the half-dark, her body other men — how many others? — had possessed. He spoke again and his voice was like ice. "You are like the Calcutta prostitutes, that too many customers have left wide open," he told her. "Stay out of my sight," for she had begun to struggle up.

"Please — "

"I want no more of you. I shall never return to Vollands, or set eyes on you again. Did I believe I loved you? I did not know then that you were a whore."

She was bewildered; he had been so tender at first, then swiftly cruel; and she had given herself as she had never done before. She heard his voice, hard, cold, suddenly that of a stranger; he had said he would marry her, and now he said he was going away and would never return. She clutched her breasts in agony.

"Listen to me," she begged. "Let me explain — "

He cracked into laughter. "Explain? Explain how you let every man in the countryside lay you on your back? Is that what you would explain?"

"No, I — "

"Then be silent. Wait here till I have returned to the house and then come in by yourself. I am ashamed lest any of my family should know I have been with you."

He turned and strode off; she lay

sobbing on the ground, covered as it was with last year's leaves. Her hands reached out and clawed it, and felt something rough and warm where he had spread it below her; his cloak. She clutched it to her, holding it against her cheek. The dark came down; when it had come Jenny crept out of the coppice, Hew's cloak held against her; made her way back to the house and went in, fearful of meeting him again, of meeting anyone at all with the stains of tears she knew were on her face. She hurried upstairs to her own room, and undressed, crying silently. Standing there she heard the sound of horses galloping off. He must have gone already, with his man.

"Hew came, but received a message that he was to return at once. They have no consideration for the officers any more than the men," complained Anna. "We scarcely saw him, except once at dinner; and how changed he is! Buckland's death meant more to him than anyone knew. And now I only have two sons at home; James, when he returns, and Mark. I would so much like to send Mark to Rugby, to Dr Arnold, about whom Christian always speaks, and who has been here twice and was most agreeable; but where are the fees to come from? I can hardly ask James, who is only now finding his feet, and has a wife and four daughters to support."

The pleading glance surveyed Mr Tillotson, who pursed his lips in the considering way he had, and wrinkled his long nose. In fact, he had been waiting, more or less patiently, for the opportunity of doing Anna a favour; that being done, he might then ask her for Juley. His interest in the young girl had developed into a passion that surprised him as the months wore on, and he was troubled lest other suitors come and oust him.

He risked everything, and said that he would pay Mark's school fees if — he added it at once — Anna would consider him as a suitor for her daughter. Anna's eyes widened, and she kept careful control of her expression. This was what she had been hoping for, and now Rugby thrown in as well! She employed her familiar gesture of stretching out a graceful hand.

"It is hard for me, my dear friend, to consider my child as old enough to marry," she told him. "But we will see. Let us send for her." She rang the little bell which sat on a table by her, to summon the maidservant, who came. "Tell Miss Julia that she is wanted in the drawing-room," Anna said.

"Madam, the Captain rode off without his cloak."

"Do as you are bid. He will send for it. Fetch Miss Julia."

Juley came, and thankfully was tidy; she was wearing a blue dress which had been made down from one of Christian's, and her pretty brown hair had been combed. She sat on the smaller sofa and said not a word, while her mother and Mr Tillotson made polite talk. After he had gone Anna looked impatiently at her daughter.

"Could you not have said something, instead of sitting there like a trussed fowl? I may tell you, though I cannot understand why, that Mr Tillotson has professed an interest in you. He is very rich, and if you play your cards carefully you will make an excellent marriage; as you know, I cannot afford to give you a season, and this may be your only opportunity."

Juley was horror-struck. That old man! She and Ocky had often laughed at him, with his spinsterish ways and long nose and pursed mouth. If she had to marry one of Mama's admirers, she would rather it were Mr Handley.

"What have you to say?" demanded Anna.

"Nothing, Mama."

Juley moved restlessly on the sofa. "Mama, Jenny is crying. She has been crying all morning. Her eyes are red."

"What is that to me?" said Anna. "Listen to me? I want you to consider this proposal seriously. When James comes home I shall discuss it with him, and certainly he will be agreeable." She bent a sudden, radiant smile on her daughter. "Think of having all the money in the world to buy whatever you want, gowns, jewels, furs, and Surtees Hall as well! You are a fortunate young woman; do not let the chance slip."

"May I go now, Mama?"

Anna waved her away. "Yes, go if

you will, by all means. Tell them to bring me a newspaper. I had not time to hear from Hew all the horrors that seem to be going on in that part of India, or is it Afghanistan? No doubt he will write. They did not say where the cloak was that he left. I expect they will discover it."

Jenny had found herself, in some way, changed. After the day's weeping her tears had dried; she was aware of a strange sensation to which she could not put a name, as though she were still herself and yet no longer what she had been: as though some process ran in her blood, changing her flesh, making her look at the world outside as if from a citadel no one could enter. There was no sign, so early, otherwise except that her breasts were already tender. There was no one to consult or to tell her what to do. In any case there was nothing to be done but wait: and with waiting would come Mr James. She loathed the thought of his return and yet knew, as if she had been told, that he was necessary, that she must go as usual at his bidding and lie with him in the great bed, more than once, perhaps often: and in the same way knew that whatever he did now would not affect her, that he could never touch her inwardly again. So she went about her tasks with the children quietly, waiting; they had not noticed her red eyes. And the nights, in her own room, brought comfort, because she could wrap Hew's cloak about her; during the day she kept it hidden beneath the covers. The bitter way in which it had been left meant less to her than its rough warmth, the awareness that it had hung from his shoulders, close to his body, both in far places and at home in England. He would never return to claim it; he had not meant to leave it to solace her; but she clung to it, and whenever it was against her, thought of him.

James was delayed for a few days by a cogent reason; he had made an appointment to see Sir Henry Halford, the royal physician, to ascertain that there was nothing amiss with his own powers of procreation. Sir Henry was in the country for a few days, and James had to wait, which he did with patience, because the thoughts of being examined by the man who had prescribed for the last three Kings of England flattered him. Old Sailor Billy, George IV, and their unfortunate father had all been treated for their various ailments by Sir Henry; and the latter had yet another distinction. When James had dropped the great man's name to an acquaintance at his club, the latter launched forth into a history which did not interest his hearer very much, as it did not concern James directly. "You will know, of course, that Sir Henry helped to identify the body of Charles I at Windsor when they opened the coffin," the other said. "That will be more than twenty years ago now. The Martyr King was perfectly recognisable, I understand, with one eye partly open. Sir Henry likes, I believe, to discourse on it, if you were to ask him. He is not very well, which is hardly surprising when one considers his age. Many men would have retired, but his work is his life: he comes to London as often as he can."

James set out to persuade Sir Henry to

work on his constitution. He was shown into a prosperous consulting-room with velvet curtains draped across the windows, and a conversation-couch to accommodate patients. He perched himself on it, and presently Sir Henry entered. Anyone but James would have felt the great weight of history in the presence of the old man; but James was intent on himself. He launched at once into the story of his woes; his wife could bear him only daughters, except a son who had been stillborn. Was he in some way incapable of fathering a living son?

Sir Henry examined him; the skilled hands that had touched the afflicted George III and both his sons made themselves familiar with the physiology of James Volland; his heart, lungs, kidneys, digestion, reproductive parts. A specimen of semen was taken for testing; Sir Henry assured James that, as his client was anxious to return to the country, the results would be with him in twenty-four hours. "We have to act quickly with sperms, in any case, or they die." He smiled, and began to dismiss James courteously; so far he had found nothing wrong with him. At the door he suddenly said a thing which might have come from his extensive experience of human nature, a stray considerate thought for the woman who had to bear this man's children. "It is not advisable to have frequent intercourse when trying for a pregnancy," he said. "Leave the embryo to settle; do not disturb it. If the first attempt fails, then try a second, but in due course, not at once. That is the best advice I can offer you."

James returned to his club, waited for the result of the sperm test, which was normal; paid the accompanying bill, which was large; and returned to the country. On the way he anticipated the following night with Jenny. He would take the old physician's advice and would not send for her too frequently thereafter. It was possible in any case that she was already pregnant by him. James found himself looking forward to renewed possession of her with an eagerness foreign to his cold nature. He spent the journey planning how to act when, as must surely happen, there was a prospect of her bearing his child. In his baggage was a ring he had purchased in London. It was not made of real gold; that would have been extravagant. In any case Jenny should not have it till her pregnancy had been proved.

6

JULEY was miserable. Now that Mark had been sent off to Rugby, a little late for the beginning of term but with all his gear provided, she had been made to feel by her mother that the other half of the bargain must be completed by herself. Mr Tillotson had begun to press his attentions in an unmistakeable manner: instead of occupying his former place at her mother's feet, he would sit beside Juley on the sofa, and do everything, as Juley told Octavia, but put his arm round her waist like a courting manservant. "And Mama smiles and looks on," she told her sister. "I can't escape. They want the wedding to be in June, and Mama talks of white satin and worries about the lack of a bouquet, but expects something to be provided from the hothouses at Surtees Hall. And you are to be the bridal attendant. It is all arranged."

"It may not be as bad as you think,"

said Ocky practically. "Plenty of money will be very agreeable."

"But that old maid! *He* is not agreeable, at least not to me; and nobody has asked my opinion. He did not even propose. He and Mama assumed everything was settled. I feel like a horse or a cow, taken to market."

"Do not let Christian hear you speak so coarsely," said Octavia, who recalled her elder sister's schoolroom teachings.

"Christian! She is as much of an old maid as Mr Tillotson; and she is nearer his age than I am."

Juley suddenly got up, flounced over to the door where her old coat hung on a hook, and said she was going for a walk. "I had better come with you," said Octavia, mindful of the proprieties. "Mama would not like you to go out alone."

"I don't want anyone with me. I want to be left in peace while I can."

She went out, shutting the door behind her; and at first went up the hill towards the school, the mention of Christian having made her anxious to see her eldest sister; perhaps she would have some advice. But when Juley reached the door the maid, a Volland named Kate, told her that both headmistresses were engaged; they were showing parents round the school, and would be having tea with them privately afterwards.

Juley turned away, dejected; it was cold, and her coat and shoes were thin. She did not want to go home yet, and turned instead towards a little beech-wood where next month there would be a mist of bluebells, and birds would have made their nests in the silver boles of the trees. But instead of looking for signs of them Juley sat down on a fallen trunk and wept. It took a long time for all the tears to come. At home there was neither privacy nor freedom; Ocky shared her room. Ocky was practical, no doubt, with her feet on the ground; but it was useless to expect either sympathy or understanding from her. The tears flowed on; then a man's voice spoke, a gentle voice, full and deep.

"It is Miss Julia, is it not? You are in some trouble or distress; may I not help you if I can?"

It was the drawing-master, Mr Byrne;

she had often thought of him. She smiled through her tears, and he knelt down on the ground and dried her eyes with his large white handkerchief. Juley found him good to look at, much better than Mr Tillotson. Even the black hair receding a little from his forehead she found attractive; beneath it, his face was beautiful. She began to tell him the things that were wrong; how she was being made to marry Mr Tillotson because her brother had been sent by him to school; how nobody would listen, and her elder sister could not see her, "not that she would sympathise either; everyone says it is an excellent match and that there will be plenty of money. I don't care about money. But I must not trouble you with my afflictions; there is nothing to be done except endure them, and be thankful if I can."

"You cannot," he told her. "It is a most monstrous thing. They must not force you into a marriage you detest."

"You know Mr Tillotson?" It was reassuring to find someone who agreed with her. He nodded, still on his knees on the ground. Some small animal, a squirrel or mouse, rustled among the moss nearby.

"He is one of the school donors," Tom Byrne said. "I have met him, accordingly."

"Do you like it at the school?"

She had blinked away her tears, and was prepared to take an interest in him, as he had taken it in her. Byrne grimaced a little.

"I endure it," he told her. "There is very little talent, and teaching young ladies can, for a bachelor, as you once pointed out, be trying."

"You mean they try to flirt with you," said Juley. Mr Byrne's sensitive mouth twisted into a rueful smile. "Some are worse than others," he told her. "When I can, I escape to places like this wood, to draw." He had a folder of sketching-gear with him, which he had laid down on the ground.

"I am glad you came to the wood," Juley said. "You have made me feel better."

"I have done very little, I fear. Shall we meet here again? I would like you to feel that you have a friend, to whom you may talk; who may, if it can be done, help you in this situation. Would you allow me to do so?"

She felt the colour rising in her cheeks. "If you will, it would be most kind. But the wedding is in six weeks' time. That is not so very far away. If I were clever, I would run away and obtain a post as governess, but I know too little."

"June is also the end of term here," he said. He was looking at her intently. "Will you believe that I have not forgotten my promise to be of help? At any time, you know where to find me; but any communication had best remain secret."

He helped her up from the log, for it was growing dark as well as somewhat cold; and gave her his arm till they reached the path. "I cannot thank you enough," said Juley. "You have cheered me, and I thought I would never be cheerful again."

He smiled down, though his height was not much greater than her own. Then they went their separate ways; she understood that it was not advisable for him to be seen with her, emerging from a beech-wood in spring.

James's eldest daughter Anna Belinda had a noticing nature: she could not remember a time when she had not perceived things and kept them to herself. The reason for the latter course was that nobody would listen to her, or else she was whipped or scolded for making known her thoughts, so she no longer made them known. Her mother, she knew, was not interested in her; Maud's visits to the nursery were like those of a stranger, and it was a relief when she went away. Her father Anna Belinda disliked. Everything about him, his little prim mouth, his moustache, his neatly tailored clothes, his manners, were obnoxious. When she heard that he was returning home, it brought the child no pleasure. She heard his carriage wheels outside the door, and the sounds of his arrival, and watched Jenny, who was sewing, and went on sewing; it did not seem as if she were at all excited about the return of Papa. Time passed, and there was nursery tea; the same as always, bread and butter, or jam instead of butter; never both; a variety of fruit cake in which the cook, who had come after Aunt Pippa went away, excelled, or thought she did; it was doughy and indigestible, but judged to be a treat. There was milk to drink, and Jenny was allowed milky tea. That was that, and afterwards Anna Belinda's immense energy was allowed to spend itself in looking after her sisters, which meant seeing that Maudie did not fall on the floor and that Beatrice, if she wet her drawers as still happened, was given a clean diaper. As for Adela, she was not any more interesting than the dolls Anna Belinda detested.

She herself was an ungainly child, with her large bones and legs and arms which she could not seem to use gracefully. Her hair, as so often with the Vollands, was her only beauty, but its colour meant a lack of visible eyebrows which made her cheekbones stick unredeemed out of her face. If anyone had been interested in the lively mind which lay behind the plainness, they would have been rewarded; but no one took any heed. Certainly Anna Belinda's father, putting in an appearance in the nursery before the children went to bed, ignored her. He had eyes only for

Jenny, who stood wordlessly, her eyelids cast down like a nun's. She was wearing a dark dress and still held her sewing.

"You will come downstairs tonight," Anna Belinda heard her father say. Jenny gave no sign, except for a slight firming of the lips. James turned and went out. Anna Belinda went up to Jenny, whom she trusted and almost loved, except that it was unsafe to love anyone.

"Where are you going tonight, downstairs? I heard Papa say it."

The eyelids raised themselves, revealing Jenny's eyes, suddenly cold as winter lakes. Anna Belinda was aware of a strange sensation, as if she were in the presence of someone she did not know.

"Nowhere that is important," was the reply. "And now it is time you went to bed."

Nowhere important; that was how she thought of it now; yet, if Hew's child was to be protected, all-important. She was sure now. This morning, for the first time, she had felt sick for no reason. There had been scant leisure for certainty except that in her mind she was indeed certain, had been so from the beginning, almost from the moment of conception in the coppice. To have given herself wholly, as she had done, to Hew; to have received his seed; that had made a child between them. Anything she did now would be to ensure it a home, a guardian. Hew might never know; she herself would never tell him. Yet this child was more precious than gold. James would not disturb it tonight where it lay, or any night; nothing he did to her must be allowed to matter, but, for the child's sake, she must go to him.

Nowhere important. She found her way as usual and saw him lying in bed waiting for her to undress, his narrow chest covered with silver-fair hair. She undressed, and the rest happened, no differently, except that she knew he could not reach her secret. He in his turn felt her lie quiet and passive under him, almost like a dead woman. He endured it smugly, assuming that, as he had earlier told himself, she would grow accustomed in time to the intensity of his urgings. One thing irritated him; afterwards, when she was dressing herself again, she turned her back on him. He almost called out to her, then thought better of it; after all, he could console himself with the assurance that he had mated her thoroughly tonight. The results remained to be seen; meantime, as Sir Henry had said, he must allow matters a reasonable time to settle.

"You need not come tomorrow," he called after her, "or until I send for you again."

He lay back on his comfortable pillow, secure in the remembrance of enjoyment. Despite everything he half hoped that it would be necessary to send for Jenny again soon. He had missed her in London.

Jenny let him send for her three times. She had developed a new cunning, like an animal, and she would sooner endure James and his embraces than give him grounds for suspicion that the child was not his. As it was, autumn had gone and winter began before she was able to say to him, the next time he demanded that she come to him, "I am going to have a child."

She spoke calmly. He leaned towards her from the bed, light eyes eager, surveying her body; she had not taken off her dress. He asked her questions, which she answered coldly; had she missed a period? More than one? She said she was uncertain. Had she been sick in the mornings? Occasionally.

"You do not show it. Come here."

She went to him passively and let him feel her breasts, which had swelled till her bodice was tight. He fondled them and her arms, kissed her, and stroked her neck. "Make it a boy, Jenny," he said. Then he put her from him. "I have some instructions for you," he told her. "Go to the box on my table there, and open it; inside you will find a wedding ring. Put it on."

She obeyed, asking no questions; the less she said the more certain it was that he would look after her and the baby. The ring was loose on her finger; she turned it about.

"We will buy a guard for it," he said. "Now I want you to listen to me. You were married in the course of the year to a soldier who is abroad on active service. Meantime you will be seen as little as possible. You may stay upstairs instead of going to the nursery; food will be sent to you. I will employ someone else to look after the children. Everything must be done to ensure that this child is born alive and healthy. Thereafter he will be known as mine; the whys and wherefores of the situation need not trouble you. Do you understand what you are to do? Can you play your part?"

She thought so, she told him flatly. Within herself she wondered how, if the child was a soldier's — her eyes shut in an instant's agony — it was also that of James. He could work that out for himself. She would be left in peace upstairs, with no more visits to or from him: that suited her.

"You may go now, Jenny," said James unctuously. "I shall not require you tonight."

He was less obsequious to Maud, next day; he issued orders as though she had been a servant. She had been sitting alone in the back room she used when Anna, in the drawing-room, did not seek out her company. She was doing nothing, her hands slack in her lap. A more unattractive woman could hardly be imagined; shapeless with childbearing, her hair in need of washing and screwed up with pins, her eyes red-rimmed and vacant. He looked at her with distaste. Maud shifted uncomfortably; what did he want with her? He seldom came in here; it was a place she could have to herself. Since Edith's death last year she did not care for company.

"Can you not find yourself some occupation?" asked James coldly. Maud did not answer; her eyes slewed round to survey him where he stood. When he began to speak she listened incredulously.

"Julia's wedding is to take place next week. You will let it be known, discreetly, that you are again in a delicate situation. We are both aware that this is not so. You have failed as a wife in every way; you will accordingly carry out my wishes now. Your figure — " he cast a contemptuous glance over it as she sat — "will lend credence to that, or to any, story. You could perhaps assist the fiction with a shawl, or later on even a pillow. At the appropriate date you will be brought to bed. The rest you may leave to me. Are your proceedings clear?"

Her mouth had fallen open, showing the gaps where she had lost teeth; she looked almost witless. Something wicked was going on, she knew; but there was nothing she could do, nothing she ever had been able to do, to oppose James. She tried to speak and managed a croak, unlike her everyday voice, to ask what about Mrs Anna; would she be told?

"You may leave my mother to me. There is another matter. During the year, Jenny Volland was married. I was one of the few persons informed of the incident. She is now expecting a child. I am informing you of it lest there should be any unpleasantness or ill-treatment of Jenny when her state becomes apparent. That is all, and you will act with discretion in both matters; remember, the wedding is the time to spread the news, but always with discretion."

She looked after him as he went out, and her expression was no longer so witless as it had been; there was malevolence in the red-rimmed eyes. So that little harlot Jenny was pregnant, and James thought the child was his! But she, Maud, had seen a thing nobody else had done, from her window while James was away last autumn; two lovers, Hew and Jenny, with their arms about one another, going from the house to the coppice, on a misty evening in late autumn. Maud had hidden herself behind the curtain, and watched; and had seen Hew come back alone in the end, and later ride away. It would be a jest, the only one in her whole life, if James were to father Hew's son. She would accordingly do everything she could to aid Jenny, pillow and all; and the child at last brought down to be passed off as her own. No doubt he would pretend Jenny's child was dead.

The room was cold. Maud started walking up and down it, not liking to ask for a fire to be lit. This had never been a house in which she was mistress: it was always Mrs Anna.

That lady received James's news lightly, even the information about Jenny's marriage. "Who was the clergyman?" she asked. "Was it Dr Bond?"

"You must leave all such matters to me, Mama; only do not treat Jenny as if she had transgressed, like an erring servant."

Anna yawned behind her hand. James was becoming insufferably pompous since his appointment to the vestry and his affairs in London. She wished the post would come; she was hoping against hope for a letter from Hew. He had gone out again to India, and these days wrote very seldom. Anna saw James go without any further curiosity; by now the whole house was busy preparing for the wedding, except for Maud who was of course idle; perhaps her state accounted for that. One must be charitable.

"Where is Tillotson?" asked Mr Handley, seating himself in his usual place at Anna's feet. He was somewhat behindhand with the news, having spent the past few weeks at a watering-place with his mother, who was still convalescing. He had, however, seen the announcement of the engagement in the papers, and secretly congratulated himself in that he would, henceforth, have Anna's undivided attention when he called.

Anna was smiling at him, but her

mind was elsewhere; in fact, she found Mr Handley *en seule* a bore, but his admiration, at her age, continued to flatter her. She answered absently that Mr Tillotson was no doubt supervising the changes to his house that he was having made for the impending marriage. "He has even chosen the curtains for Juley's room," she murmured, the thought crossing her mind that had Juley been more forceful or more interested, she might have resented having curtains chosen for her. Where *was* Juley? The white satin wedding dress stood ready on its dressmaker's stand upstairs; everything was prepared, and Octavia looked enchanting in her bridal attendant's dress of rose-pink organza with matching velvet ribbons. But Juley had stood like a doll to be dressed when they were pinning the white satin, and had not even looked at herself in the glass.

" — and so Mama will return later this year, for the sea-bathing, which shows great courage at her time of life. I must say I myself have never entered a machine," said Mr Handley, a trifle wistfully; when he was a boy, in fact, his Mama would not permit him to bathe because of his asthma. It no longer troubled him quite so much, but —

"There was a note left upstairs for you in our room, from Juley."

Octavia had come in, nodded to Handley — her manners were always assured — and handed her mother the note. Juley had gone off some hours ago on one of her solitary walks, from which as a rule she would have returned long ago. Octavia had happened to go to their room, and had seen the letter.

There was a gasp. Anna had excused herself to the visitor, torn open the envelope, and now was staring as if transfixed at whatever it contained. Presently she raised her head and gazed at Handley, but not as though she saw him.

"It will be all over the county soon," she said, "so you may as well hear. Julia has eloped with the drawing-master from Hubertshall. It is uncertain whether or not they are even married." She looked wildly about her. "Who is to break it to poor Mr Tillotson?" she asked of nobody in particular. "I suppose it will have to be James."

7

JAMES betook himself in the carriage to Mr Tillotson's house, which was a minor Palladian imitation based on Houghton Hall, which Tillotson in his youth had been taken to see and had always remembered. Although nowhere near the scale of that imposing edifice, Surtees House was elegant to behold, not in the most modern taste but none the worse for that. Surveying it as the wheels turned up the smooth and even drive, James reflected what a fool Juley had been to throw all this away.

Mr Tillotson himself received the news with more philosophy than might have been foreseen. Truth to tell, he had been so greatly taken up with choosing curtains that it was some time since he had paid any direct attention to his future bride. Her lack of apparent interest in him he had put down to maidenly reserve, which would be removed in the accepted fashion after marriage. He was, naturally, shocked and distressed at the news of her elopement, but he was not brokenhearted.

He saw James off, after a glass of wine taken together and the assurance that Tillotson would not cease to visit Anna at Vollands. After bowling out again at the great gates, James did not go home; instead, he directed the coachman to Hubertshall. He had a clear awareness in his mind of what he must now do; he had already told himself that it was no less than his duty. In any case Christian would have to be informed of her sister's elopement as privately as possible.

He was more fortunate than Julia had been, and found both ladies taking tea alone. Invited to join them, James declined; he preferred to stand, portentous and full of news, with a frown on his face that would have chilled Maud to the marrow, but disturbed neither Christian nor Ellen.

"What is the matter, James?" enquired his sister. She was wearing a prune-coloured gown, and looked very striking. It was always a matter for wonder to visiting parents that so handsome a woman as Miss Volland had never married. James bent his brows upon her, and told her in a few words why there would be no wedding.

"But how wicked! The wickedness of it!" It was Ellen who was upset, not Christian. "He — Byrne — told us at the end of last term that he was leaving, as he had found another situation, and asked for references. We gave them — did you not, Christian? — as he had been an adequate teacher, if not inspired. Had we known this was to happen, of course nothing of the kind would have been provided."

"Do you know which school has agreed to employ him?" James asked her.

Ellen thought for a moment, then said, "Yes, I think so. He left an address for forwarding letters, and it was that of a school. If you will excuse me for a moment, I will search in my desk."

She rose and went out. Christian said, "Are you going to write to the school, James? It will lose him his situation, and he and Julia may be in dire straits without money."

"They should have thought of that before, should they not? A good deal of money has been spent — and wasted

— over the wedding." James pursed his mouth; he would have to meet the bills, and Anna's enthusiasm over the rich marriage had ensured that they would not be small.

Ellen returned, a piece of paper in her hand, which she handed to James. It contained the address of a not very well known girls' school which, however, would pay Byrne a salary.

James scanned it, his mouth tightening still further. "I will keep this, if I may," he said. In fact he knew, and both women knew also, that he might keep anything he chose; here, as well, he paid the bills.

"We know that you will act correctly," said Ellen. Christian said nothing. She felt that matters should have been left as they were; of what purpose was it to render Byrne incapable of supporting a wife? Aloud she said, however, "This must not become known in the school. Any breath of scandal would reflect on us. Parents might remove the girls."

"He must have been meeting her from here all the time," said Ellen indignantly. Christian watched her, wondering why she was so vindictive at the mention of the lovers. She herself had no feelings; and having seen Tillotson, could understand why Juley had run away from so old and unattractive a bridegroom. It had been a mistake of Mama's to try to force the marriage.

Vollands, 1st July 1841
The Headmistress,
Locksley Wick School for Girls,
Hackney, London.

Madam,
Although I will be totally unknown to you, I venture to write on a subject that concerns you deeply. I am a governor of Hubertshall school, where until recently a Mr Thomas Byrne was employed as drawing-master. I believe that he acquired references which no doubt enabled him to obtain a similar appointment with yourself, to begin in September. I must mention that Mr Byrne has recently eloped with a young woman whom he may or may not have married, and that if his former employers had been apprised of this fact in time there would have been no references given to him. I leave it to

139

your own good sense to decide what to do, but were I in your shoes I would hesitate to employ, especially among young girls, a person who has behaved in such a manner.

I trust that this information will be of use to you, and am, madam,

Your devoted servant,
James Volland

Locksley Wick School,
7th August 1841

Dear Mr Volland,

I am more grateful than I can say for your letter of last month and for the information with which you furnished me about the character of the man we had thought to employ. Needless to say, he has been dismissed without a reference. He will find it extremely difficult to obtain another situation at this time of year, and without guarantors.

I have heard of Hubertshall and of the excellent quality of its teaching, and congratulate you on your governorship of so worthy an institution.

Yours very sincerely,
Bertha Bright, Headmistress

140

Meantime, another letter had gone out from Vollands. It was addressed to Surtees Hall.

3rd August 1841

Dear Mr Tillotson,

I did not send you my condolences at the time of the expected wedding, as it would not have been proper. No doubt this letter is improper also. If you think so, and would prefer to destroy it, its contents need never be mentioned again.

I know that my sister Julia had an interest elsewhere. I have none. Apart from yourself and Mr Handley, Squire Fielding — have you heard that he is lately married again? — and my brothers, I am not acquainted with any gentlemen, and do not look likely to meet any, as we never go out into the world.

If you would like it, I am prepared to marry you. I think I would make as good a wife as anybody else; I have not had the practice in cookery of my sister Pippa, nor am I clever like my sister Christian. I have, however, common sense, and some wit, and like yourself I appreciate beautiful things. I have heard *of Surtees Hall although I have never been there, and I would engage to make a good mistress to it and a good wife to you.*

My only other fate is to become a companion to Mama, and although she is charming and attracts much admiration, it is not a prospect which any young woman would desire for herself while she grows old. Otherwise I must look after my nieces. I would rather have children of my own.

As I say, there is no need to reply to this letter or take heed of it, if you do not choose to do so.

Yours sincerely,
Octavia Volland

James was uncomfortable. He had not had a woman lately; not since he had instructed Jenny to take herself upstairs as no longer required. It was however three months till her child should be born, and containing himself until then would be difficult and unpleasant. Afterwards — he contented himself with looking forward to the future — Jenny should be his mistress again; but it was of such importance that his son should be born with every advantage that he would not touch her meantime. She was thickening agreeably; he saw her from time to time, passing along the corridors.

A little maid named Annie Volland had been exchanged from Hubertshall, and came in daily to James's study to clean out the grate and lay the fire. She was a mousy little creature, not of the calibre of Jenny; but she was a woman. One day when she came James locked the door, and when Annie had finished her task waylaid her, and tried to persuade her towards the sofa. To his annoyance, Annie began to scream aloud. She would by no means lie down under him. She screamed until, perforce, he undid the lock; and let her go, concealing himself prudently inside the room; Annie ran out of the house, up the hill to Hubertshall, and told everyone she met that she would not go back to Vollands, and why; exactly the situation James had wished to avoid. Later in the day he was confronted by her brother George, a bull-like young man, not very tall, but with fists like hams.

"You lay hands on our Annie again,

and I'll smash yer face in."

James essayed a display of authority. "Do not address me in such a way, my good fellow; take yourself off. I can have you arrested for threatening, and I will do so."

"Arrested, eh? What's happened to Jenny? We never heard tell of any marriage. Where is she? Who's seen her? If you ask me, you've been at her as well."

"You may see Jenny if you wish," said James coldly.

She came, while the young man straddled the carpet meaningfully; and stood quiet, till she heard what it was that they wanted. Her body was thick against the stuff of her gown; she had a placid look. When asked, she held out her hand with the wedding ring on it.

"Are you satisfied now?" said James.

"Ay. I dare say. Is it all right, Jenny? It's a long time since you left us."

Jenny said it was all right, and George went away. Later that night James perforce visited his wife, as there was no other alternative.

Octavia was walking in the garden next day with James's daughters. They were a spiritless lot, except for Anna Belinda, who ran back and forth to use up her energy; as a rule Ocky would have rebuked her sharply, but at present her mind was elsewhere. By now, Mr Tillotson would certainly have received her letter. Had she behaved improperly? It was possible; and that meant years and years of sitting by Mama while he and Handley paid court to her and ignored oneself despite everything, which would be most humiliating. Yet prudence — Octavia had her share of James's qualities — had its disadvantages in that had she not written, nothing would ever have happened one way or the other. If —

Anna Belinda cannonaded against her knee. "Oh, do be quiet," snapped Octavia, and gave the child's cheek a slap. Anna Belinda did not cry; she was used to slaps, whippings, boxed ears, punishments. Everybody expected one to keep quiet, not to be noticed, not to think or speak. There was somebody coming across the lawn now, but she would say nothing about it in case it was considered wrong to do so. It was a tall thin man, the one who came sometimes to see Grandmama.

Something made Octavia turn her head. She blushed, the rosy colour in her cheeks heightening becomingly. Bartholomew Tillotson removed his hat, the light wind blowing the thinning hair about his half-bald scalp. But his eyes were those of a young man today, shining and grateful.

"My dear Octavia," he said, "I came at once."

The wedding took place quietly, not in church, but in Mrs Anna's drawing-room at Vollands. The single bridal attendant was Anna Belinda, released for the day from durance in the form of the hired nursemaid who had been brought in some time since to replace Jenny. There were no guests apart from the immediate family, and the extravagant preparations for the previous ceremony were not repeated. There was cake and wine, and then the couple left for a honeymoon in Paris, concerning which the bride had been heard to announce that it didn't matter about the lack of a trousseau; Bart would buy her all the gowns she wanted from famous dressmakers at the Palais Royal. It was evident that this was a happier occasion than the last would have been; only Anna was left in bewilderment as to how it had happened at all. Mr Handley, also, was as wistful as he had been over the bathing-machine: he would have liked little Ocky for himself, at some time in the future, when Mama and her problems were out of the way; but that had not happened yet.

Jenny had been able, during the summer weather, to walk about in the grounds in early morning, when she would meet nobody. The rest of the day she spent idly, for she was forbidden by James to appear, and there was nothing to do but lie on her bed, or sit in a chair. As the months passed she watched her body change and grow heavier, and she had to loosen her laces more and more. She would have liked to sew clothes for the baby, but had neither needles nor stuff, and neither Mrs Anna nor Mrs Maud would have been likely to provide them for her. However rescue was at hand, while she stayed, from Annie Volland. Their sister Grace had married a farm-worker, had had a little girl last year and was shortly expecting another. Annie appeared at Jenny's door one day with used clothes, needles, and cut-out stuff. The last was in flannel, and would be useful for the winter; the baby was due in November. Jenny cried out in thanks.

"Tell Grace I'll do something for her, one day," she cried. Annie looked at her quizzically.

"You haven't been much about us Vollands, have you? Might not be a sister at all. Might be from here, except that they don't trouble with you. Who's going to be with you when it's born? Can't have it by yourself; someone has to be there to cut the cord and wash the baby." Annie had experience from her other sisters, who were all married except herself.

Jenny said she didn't know. Fretting over who was going to be here hadn't occurred to her. The birth would come, and the child would live; something had told her that from the beginning.

She set herself to sewing up the small

flannel garments, to pass her days; when something even stranger happened.

The October trees had shed their leaves, which drifted down on to the lawn, brown and red; and old Matthew the scything man swept them up with a birch-twig broom, and burned them; the smoke drifted past the windows. All Souls' Eve came and passed, and then it was November; and at night Jenny was alone in her room, the day's sewing put away for lack of light. She had begun to undo her gown, moving clumsily because of her distended body, by now almost at term. Then she heard a voice speak to her, and it was Hew's.

"Jenny. Little Jenny."

He was in the room with her; somewhere, unseen, untouched, only sensed, and well remembered. Whatever anger had seared him was gone; she knew that he understood, that he no longer blamed her. She knew also, without having to be told, that he was dead.

The news came two months later to Mrs Anna while she was reading other letters. Maud was with her; there was nobody else to sit with Anna now. Maud had a certain preening self-satisfaction about her these days; afraid as she was of her husband, it was a triumph, in any woman's terms, that he came and slept with her every night. She watched while Anna opened the army despatch. It was a long time since they had heard from Hew, who was in Kabul.

Anna gave a gasp. Two British envoys had been murdered; but that was not all. Upon terms of a safe escort to India, the garrison had marched out; and were massacred almost to a man. One, only one, a doctor named Brydon, came home, having survived hunger, exposure, and danger. Hew himself was long dead. It was thought that he had perished in the earlier revolt at Kabul in November.

Maud saw Anna stand still and tall. "I had five sons," she heard her say. "They were fine comely boys, fine men. Now there are only James and Mark left."

She turned away, and went to her own room. She had not shed a tear, but from that day she became an old woman.

By then, Jenny had had her baby.

To everyone's surprise, James had ordered the services of a doctor and a midwife. This was more than he had done for any of his daughters; more in fact than had ever been done for Mrs Anna herself when she was giving birth to her own children. Eyebrows were raised, notably those of Mrs Octavia Tillotson, by then herself in a promising situation. She was visiting her mother at the time of the birth, having arrived in a new dark-green chaise her husband had given her as a sign of his pleasure at her pregnancy and her wifeliness in general. She was becomingly dressed, had put on weight, and altogether resembled a young woman who had been married for years, so well did the state suit her. While Jenny laboured upstairs, Maud, Ocky and Anna sat downstairs, drinking marsala and commenting on the situation. James was in his study and did not join them.

The doctor was pleased with Jenny: a gentle and obedient young woman who gave no trouble and did not, as so many did, rend the air with crying out beyond the necessary. The child was normally placed and should come soon; he was certain of his fees from Mr Volland, and had no objection, although his time was valuable, to waiting here until the baby was born. He stood and looked down at the girl straining on the bed: where was the father? If it were merely a question of a servant who had misbehaved, he himself would not have been sent for. There was more to it; but what it might be was outside his province. His duty was to see the birth safely over, and to order the midwife, who however knew her business, accordingly.

She moved towards the bed, felt Jenny, and said, "The head won't be long." This worst part of any birth Jenny accepted with patience, only biting her lip and turning her head aside in its linen cap; they had put that on her, for some new-fangled reason, and her hair was hidden. "Bear down, dear," said the midwife, and Jenny did her best; but it took an hour for the head to come, and then they pressed on it and seemed to delay the baby's birth; she wondered why, but with no sharp interest; she herself was in a place that was not this room at all, a place no one could describe, except that it would lead on to another, better place, where she wanted to go as soon as Hew's son was born. And born he was, at last: and they held him up, so that Jenny could see his head of dark hair. She smiled.

James Volland was outside; he had been kept informed by his own request, and knew that a boy had been born. He knocked for admittance, and the doctor went to the door; James thrust past him to look at the child, washed now and wrapped, lying in its mother's bed. The midwife was still seeing to Jenny.

James stared at the baby. It had Hew's features. It was true that Hew was his brother and a likeness was acceptable, but — He went to the bed, and shook Jenny by the shoulders.

"Is this my son? Is it? Tell me the truth. Answer me." There had been that one day, only one, when Hew had been home, and he himself away. Could it have happened then, in so short a time? The little bitch —

The midwife gave a shocked exclamation;

such a way to treat a woman newly delivered!

Jenny did not answer. Her eyes, veiled by their long lashes, were gazing at somebody and something near the door; something that brought her infinite, quiet joy.

The doctor came over and took James by the arm.

"She will not answer any more," he said gently. "She is dead. I do not know why. She was a healthy young woman, and the birth was normal."

James's mouth fell open beneath his moustache. He stared at Jenny, then at his possible son. It would make him look foolish to doubt that it was his. Maud would not dare mock him in his presence, but she would do so in his absence; and the news might spread. He would adopt the baby, as he had planned to do. Meanwhile, poor Jenny —

"We must make arrangements for the burial," he said prosaically. He turned and went out of the room, the doctor following. The midwife began to prepare the dead girl in the customary way, and close her eyes.

Part Two

1

JULEY stepped out of the public coach and wrapped her coat about her against the cold spring wind. The coat was the same as the one in which she had left, and was almost threadbare about her thin figure. Her shoes were worn through at the soles, and there had been no money to repair them; but she trudged on, along the familiar way that led to Vollands.

Before the house came in sight, she went over in her mind all that had happened since she left. It had begun, she thought, afterwards with Tom white and shaking, having received a letter from Locksley Wick School to say that his services would not after all be required. "It is wicked," she had told him. "What reason do they give?"

"They do not have to give any reason. I imagine someone may have written to do us harm. I will try elsewhere." But elsewhere, by so far an advanced date in the summer, had yielded no results; it would be assumed that something must be very wrong with this Mr Byrne that he had no occupation arranged for himself by now. The autumn had come, and still there was nothing; and they had slept in one another's arms in the bitterly cold attic which was all Tom could afford to rent, and presently could not afford even that. They had been out on the street then; and slept, again, close against one another in doorways, till winter came.

She had been of little help to him, she knew. A different woman would have found herself a situation, and Juley had tried; but a draper's shop, which was all she had any hope of, had insisted that she board in its hostelry, and she was not prepared to desert Tom. Governessing was out of the question, as she had known in any case; she was not sufficiently well educated, and had no references, any more than he.

Tom eventually found work heaving beer barrels out of cellars into a main drinking-parlour near the river. He would return exhausted at the end of each day, and his delicate hands, that could draw so beautifully, became calloused and hardened with the work. Presently he fell ill, and began to cough; and at that point Juley decided that she was of no use to him, and would go home meantime. "It would have been better for you if you had never met me," she told him: and remembered his pale face looking up at her from the mattress on which he lay, trying to smile. "To have met you has been the whole of my life," he whispered. She would always remember that. "Don't lose heart," she whispered. "My family will surely help us."

They kissed, clung together, and she went. She had left what money she had with a woman who would nurse him and see that he was fed. She herself had sold a little brooch Buckland had once given her for her birthday, and that helped with the fare. She could not bring herself to sit up on the coach roof among the cheapest, noisiest, probably familiar passengers, and it cost more to travel inside. Juley made up for this by not eating on the journey: by the time she got off near Vollands, she was faint with hunger.

She walked up the drive. The door was open and she went in, and turned the handle into Anna's drawing-room. Mama was alone, except for Maud. They were as Juley always remembered them, one lying on the chaise-longue, the other seated bolt upright on the small sofa. At sight of her, Maud flung up her hands.

"How dare you show yourself here?" said Anna. She could be regal from the position in which she lay, her still magnificent eyes wide open in anger. "You had better hide yourself," she said. "Octavia and Tillotson are coming, and he must on no account see you. Go into the nursery."

Maud, wordless, shoved her out of the door; Juley stumbled upstairs to where the four small girls played with their dolls, and a dark-haired baby lay in a cradle, a nursemaid by him. Juley glanced down at the baby, and presently heard the sound of wheels. Going to the window, she saw a well-kept dark green carriage bowl up, and Octavia, prosperous in furs, handed out by Tillotson. They went into the house, and Juley waited where she was; Mama was right, her jilted bridegroom must not encounter her. If only she might ask for something to eat!

She stared at the children, who stared back: Anna Belinda said, "You are Aunt Julia," with certainty, but made no other advance. Presently she smiled; someone had come into the nursery. Juley turned, and beheld Octavia. The latter's brown eyes were cold.

"I said that I would come to look at the baby," she said, "and Maud told me that you were here." She went to the cradle, and gazed down. "James intends to adopt this child," she remarked. She was like someone making conversation with a stranger.

"Will you help me, Ocky?" Juley said. "Tom is very ill. He lost his situation, and could not get another. I came here in the hope that someone would help us. A very little money would do. Later, when he is better, he will try again for work." She could hear her own voice, almost whining like a beggar's. Octavia's expression did not change.

"Why should we help you? You hurt Bartholomew very much. Your present situation is entirely your own fault."

Juley refrained from replying that it was because she had hurt Mr Tillotson that Octavia had been enabled to marry him. She had had no news from her family at all, and she and Byrne had not been able to afford the gazettes; but from the sight of the carriage, and what the others had said, not to mention the evident fact that Octavia was in a hopeful situation, it was possible to put two and two together. She firmed her lips over her sister's refusal to help. It would be necessary to ask Mama again, or James.

"James will be through shortly, and he will not be at all pleased to see you," Ocky said. "In his position he dislikes being made a fool of. You will receive no help from him."

"I will ask him, nevertheless. He may not be as hard as you are," said Juley, roundly. "We were sisters together, near of an age; nobody would think so to hear you now."

"That is all I have to say," replied Octavia, and turned and went out. Julia sat out on the stairs till she heard the couple go. Then she made her way down, and again faced Anna. James had come in meantime, and stared at her coldly.

"Did this man marry you?" was all he

said. Julia flushed.

"We had not the money for the licence," she explained. "Tom would have saved it from his first salary, but the appointment was cancelled, and since then — " She would have gone on with a recital of what their life had been, but James interrupted her with a horrified exclamation.

"Then you are a kept woman, a whore? I wonder that you dare face Mama. Leave this house immediately."

"Do you want me to go, Mama?" said Juley.

"I never want to set eyes on you again. To think that a daughter of mine would behave in such a way! I could never hold up my head again if it were known."

"May I please have some food before I go? I have eaten nothing since London, and I do not know where I am expected to go next."

"You may find what you can in the kitchen," said Anna coldly.

She went there, and was able to have a little bread and some soup, which simmered on the stove. On her way out, Maud was waiting. Juley expected further revilements, but to her surprise

James's wife whispered quickly, "Try the school. Try Hubertshall. They need a sewing-maid. If you do not say openly to everyone who you are, Ellen might employ you."

Juley thanked her; and watched her disappear, as if afraid James would glimpse her even here, even for a moment. The whole house, including Mama, seemed to be in thrall to James. No doubt that was why Mama had had to be so harsh.

Ellen and Christian were walking about the place which during the year became the girls' gardens. Although certain parents had written and objected that their daughters were being put to rough, unladylike work, it had been decided to continue with the practice. The ground had been dug over, accordingly, for the frosts to break up the earth. The brown and rimed silver made a pattern which Tom Byrne's eyes would have noted, had he been here.

The two women wore warm pelisses, and were startled to see approaching a thin, shabbily clad figure, possibly a vagrant. They straightened from examination of the beds, and prepared to send the woman about her business. Fortunately the half-term holiday had started and the girls were away.

"What do you want?" called Ellen, expecting a whined demand for money or clothes. To her astonishment the woman came forward, moving with a certain grace. It was then that Christian gave a gasp; she had recognised Juley, hollow-cheeked, undernourished, ill-clad as she was. Even her hair, which had used to be a pretty, shining brown, was brittle and lifeless. What had become of her since she left them?

"Julia." They faced one another, the prosperous headmistress in her fur pelisse and muff, her bonnet of ruched velvet for going outside; and the unfortunate younger sister, who stared for moments and then said, "I understand you need a sewing-maid. Will you employ me?"

Afterwards they wondered if they had been wise. It was agreed between them that James must not be told; his verdict would be all too predictable. Julia must keep herself upstairs in the sewing-room as much as possible, and might take exercise only in the early morning, when nobody was about. The fact that she was Christian's sister must likewise be suppressed; parents would most certainly not approve. Ellen, on the other hand, was not without kindness; she gave the poor creature a pair of her own shoes, which were not broken, and some warm flannel underwear. For the sake of respectability a black dress was provided, and Juley wore a cap and apron for her duties.

She sat diligently sewing and mending, and seemed not to desire any other life; but in fact her earnings, when she was paid them, went straight to Tom. She managed to obtain paper to write to him; she did her best to cheer him and to promise that soon, in some way, it would be possible to bring him here, or somewhere nearby.

The bastard Vollands, now ageing, came into her life, for almost the first time; Anna had never encouraged them. There was George, who had Uncle Hubert's gargantuan appetites and drank more than would have been good for any other man, but it seemed to do him no harm. He had eyed Juley at the beginning, but she had repulsed him coldly; had she made a friend of him, he would have helped her. But she was too greatly filled with anxiety about Tom to have eyes, or time, for any other man.

Most of the Volland women, except Annie, were married. Annie also would have made a friend of Julia, who had to share her room. But at night Juley turned over and pretended to be asleep, and Annie could seldom exchange a word with her; she told George, to whom she was always close, that that Julia thought she was somebody when in fact she was nobody, sitting there sewing and patching all day. As George would have agreed, there was no bond established between Juley and the Vollands; on her day off she did not go out, but spent the time in writing to Tom. The girls came back, and there was more to do in the way of work, mending torn petticoats, picking up stitches from knitted garments that had been unravelled by catching on a hook or nail; inevitably, darning stockings. As the nights lightened it was no longer necessary to peer at these, for Juley's eyes had at first grown red at the task. She longed for Tom with every fibre of her being; he seemed very far away.

James had made several influential acquaintances by his prudent conduct. The vestry meetings had led on to others; far from being satisfied with an invitation to become a Justice of the Peace, he had set his sights on London. That year his hopes were fulfilled; he was invited to become a member of the board of a merchant bank in Threadneedle Street. Naturally he accepted, and found himself a commodious flat not far from Piccadilly, in which henceforth he spent most of his time, and seldom went home, although he saw to it that the expenses of Vollands were met, having first been gone over minutely by himself. It gave him great pleasure to resign from the vestry, saying with truth that his other commitments left him no time to come down to the country on Sundays.

The commitments included a mistress, of whom James had stood for some time in much need. He found her, ironically, in the same draper's establishment where poor Juley had tried to obtain a position: at the glove counter. She was a hard-faced young woman who for some reason attracted James, and when, drawing on one of the gloves he had bought, he asked her if she would have supper with him, she shied away.

"Ow, they're very strict. If I was having supper with a gentleman I'd have to explain why."

"Then do so," said James, offering to have a cab at the door for her at closing time, which in the end he did. He also, before committing himself, took the precaution of having the young woman medically examined. Thereafter she fitted very well into the flat at Half Moon Street; he found it less and less necessary to go home.

A stout lady named Eliza Evans took her mentally retarded son Nigel by the hand and proceeded firmly up the path to Vollands. Unlike Juley, they had left the coach with plenty of provisions; half of a cold chicken, some hard-boiled eggs without their shells, a pound of apples, and a loaf and some butter reposed in

Mrs Evans' reticule, to be demolished on the journey back. Nevertheless she had hopes that Nigel would not be returning.

She knocked at the door, and was admitted by the maidservant, whom she remembered. "Why, Betty, you're still here," she remarked. "You never married?"

Betty did not reply; she could have done so, in order to say that there were some folk who married more than once, or ought to have done. She would have shown Eliza the way to Mrs Anna's drawing-room, but Eliza knew it already; and thrust her way onward like a great ship, still clutching her daft boy and her reticule.

Anna was as usual, and at first did not recognise Uncle Hubert's runaway mistress, so huge had the latter grown with the bearing of a second family after the first. When identities were established, Anna did not depart from custom; she offered no tea to the travellers. Eliza, not put out, stated why she had come.

"I came to see my Jenny's grave, and my Jenny's baby."

Anna looked about her. There was

nobody to show the woman where the Volland graves were, but she herself could tell her; they were in the private yard, at the back of the grounds; Jenny was buried there. "Then we'll go," said Eliza, making no effort to rise meantime; instead, she looked at Nigel. He was not a comely object; he might have been eleven years old, and his eyes had a peculiar slant; his mouth dribbled. "He's handy with coals and choppin' wood," Eliza said. "Since Evans went off to India the rest have got themselves places, here and there; but anyone as sees Nigel don't know what's in him. If I could see him settled, it'd do me good."

Anna felt herself weakening. They had only the old man who had replaced Matthew in using the scythe to bring in wood and coal, and he was getting past it; it might not be a bad idea to employ Nigel, if he was quiet and willing. "How much would he want?" she asked, knowing James would enquire.

Eliza smiled, giving a glimpse of the enchanting girl Hubert Volland had once taken to his bed. "Bless you, he wouldn't ask aught," she said, "except his food and a bed to sleep in. Would you, Nigel?"

Thus it was that Nigel Evans was employed at Vollands. Later, having visited the grave, Eliza went to the nursery, where Anna accompanied her. They looked down at the baby, crowing in his cot.

"I'm glad," said Eliza, "that it was Mr Hew she had, and not Mr James. I'd heard otherwise, but you've only got to look at the nose on him, and his hair. That's the Captain's son, not a doubt of it. I'm glad for Jenny's sake. She was the sweetest of 'em I left behind; I called my eldest by Evans after her. Graveyard mould, now, my Jenny; but she's left *him* to follow after."

Anna was silent. Anna Belinda had crept up behind them unseen. What was this strange woman saying? She herself had been jealous of the baby James Henry ever since he arrived; there was so much more fuss made of him than there had ever been of her. When Papa came, she'd tell him what the woman had said. She'd remember, and tell.

Eliza took her leave, handing the apples to Nigel to eat one by one as it suited him. They wouldn't keep anyway, not this time of year.

The time of year happened to be June, and Ellen and Christian were taking their customary walk of inspection round the girls' little plots. Some of these were successful, with sunflowers exposing their bright faces and reaching up to a tall height, and heliotrope giving forth its delicious scent, and even roses. Others grew vegetables; cabbages, parsnips, and carrots, although the latter were not successful owing to the heavy nature of the soil. Still other plots, perhaps because of disapproving parents, were hardly tended at all, and weeds flourished to the detriment of the neighbouring gardens. Ellen made the neglected plots the occasion for a homily, saying that such results were like the tares in the Bible that spoiled the growing harvest.

"Nothing succeeds without constant care; and you, Susan, and you, Margaret, have paid no attention to your gardens for weeks, but have spent the time gossiping and laughing together, while others worked."

Susan and Margaret, both daughters of prosperous manufacturers, received the reproof with downcast eyes and suitably shamed expressions; but as soon as the two headmistresses had gone on their way resumed their chatter in whispers at first, then, when it was safe, at the top of their voices. They had never had any hope of the annual prize in any case; that would go to the growers of sunflowers and roses. In any case, one's Papa paid the fees.

Ellen and Christian meantime made their way inside and towards the private drawing-room, where at this hour coffee was brought to them by one of the Vollands. The post had come, and lay ready on an occasional table which bore a silver tray. Most of it was for Christian, and there was one from Rugby. She opened that first, though it was not in Dr Arnold's familiar hand.

Ellen heard her give an exclamation, then saw that her face was white. "What is it?" she demanded. Christian did not show emotion as a rule.

"It is terrible news, the worst possible. Poor Dr Arnold is dead. He had been ill — he was always afraid of dying from heart disease like his father — and when his wife ran out of the room to fetch his children and the servants to see him, he was dead on her return. She has spared time to write to me, poor soul."

"It is certainly sad," said Ellen. "He was not so very old, surely?"

"Forty-seven. Why should God take a man like that so soon? He was a Fellow of Oriel, a fine classical scholar. He took a first at Corpus. He was writing a History of Rome, and it cannot have been finished. Only last year he was made Regius Professor of History at Oxford. All that, as well as his unceasing work as the best headmaster Rugby has ever had. He transformed it from chaos into a famous school, and he is taken before he is old. Why? Why?"

The tears were streaming down Christian's face. "Perhaps," said Ellen drily, "so that Mrs Arnold could have a respite from her yearly bearing of children. How many little Arnolds are there to provide for now? I think it is ten; further witness to his energy." She happened to have a correspondent of her own at Rugby, the wife of one

175

of the housemasters; but Mrs Foxe had not written today.

"How can you speak so?" said Christian reproachfully. She turned her head away from the coffee when it came. "I do not think that I can appear in school today," she said. "I shall go and lie down in my room."

"Do not stay there too long, or it will be spread about that you nourished an improper passion for the late Doctor."

"That remark is in the very worst of taste," said Christian coldly. She rose and went upstairs, and if anyone had been watching Ellen, left behind, they would have surprised what was very like a schoolboy grin on her face. She kept her humour to herself, but it was there. She poured her coffee and drank it.

It was that same day, much later than the post had come, that Annie Volland took a thumbed and dirtied letter upstairs to Juley, who was in the sewing-room. The girls were getting ready to go home for the summer, and there was a great deal to do; she had been busy since early morning, having only snatched a bite for a moment in the middle of the day. She received the letter dully; they'd kept it, of course, before troubling to bring it upstairs.

She opened it. Christian's news had been of a death, and this was almost as bad; Tom was very ill. *I think you had best come*, the words ran in round unformed writing, made with a blunt pencil: *he is spitting blood. He won't eat, and lies there with his head turned away.*

The sewing fell to the floor; Juley jumped up. "When did this come?" There was no date on it. They could have kept it for days, not caring. Haggard in the face, she stared at Annie Volland. Annie, with the countrywoman's habit of slowness with the post, couldn't understand the fuss.

"Today, maybe. Maybe yesterday. I don't know." She looked at the petticoat Julia had been mending, abandoned on the floor. Miss Ellen wouldn't be pleased at that. She sniffed, and went away; that Julia's business was none of hers; she had her own work to get on with.

Spitting blood. Not eating, lying there.

She must go to him, but how? She had no money for the fare, and this time no brooch to sell. She must go to Ellen and Christian, and borrow next term's wages; there was nothing else for it. They wouldn't like it, but surely they would listen.

She went to the door of the drawing-room and knocked. As good fortune would have it Ellen was alone, and could see her at once. She had almost finished the coffee which had come, and set the cup aside. "Well, Julia, what is it?" she said amiably. She was personally unaffected by Dr Arnold's death and pleased enough to continue to deal with the events of every day.

However, when she heard Juley's desperate appeal she frowned. "I may not support you in this," she said. "This man is not your husband." She had had that from Vollands, in general talk; James still did not know that his sister was here.

"We would have been husband and wife long ago, but for the lack of money. I'm his wife in all but the law. I would never have left him, except that he was ill, and

178

couldn't work. How can I let him die without going to him? If you have any pity in you, lend me the money. I'll work next term for nothing, I swear."

"No, it is unsuitable," said Ellen coldly. The door opened suddenly and Christian appeared, red-eyed. She had realised that she must come back, must take her customary place; but she was raw with weeping, and not prepared to withstand the sudden fierce attack Julia made on them both.

"So it's unsuitable, is it, that I should go to the man I love when he's dying? Have either of you old maids ever known the love of a man, ever been held in his arms, known the warmth that means, the glow that comes between you? It'll never happen to you now, and you know it; and your jealous minds try to keep me from my man, but you won't; I'll walk to London if I have to, and I'm going now."

She turned and went out, shutting the door. Christian stared at Ellen. "I hope none of the girls heard that diatribe," said Ellen coldly. "She is better gone."

They sat opposite one another in

silence, gazing at the empty coffee-cup. Outside there sounded the noise of the girls going from one class to another. At the end of term discipline was slack. Things would have to be tightened up in September.

Juley ran down the hill and along the dusty road that led to London. She felt the strength of anger bear her up; she could walk if she had to, but perhaps there would be a lift from a carter or farmer. She began to walk, realising that she had not removed her cap and apron. It didn't matter; it gave her respectability, she wouldn't be mistaken for a tinker. She passed the gates of Vollands without turning in; there would be no welcome for her there, or any money. What would happen to her in the future she did not consider; there was only one thing that mattered, and that was to get to Tom. In the delay before she received the letter he might have grown worse; she did not let her mind dwell on the worst possibility of all.

The sound of a cart creaking behind her made her turn, and signal. She had never before asked a stranger for a lift, and this man was not prepossessing; he had a red face and little hard eyes, but he was travelling in the right direction. He stopped the horse, and the cart came to a standstill.

"I am trying to get to London, to my husband who is ill," she explained. "Can you take me part of the way?"

"Ay, I'll take you."

She felt uncertain; she disliked his manner and the way he eyed her; but there was no one else on the road, and she clambered in. The back of the cart was full of turnips. He started up and they jogged on a little way, until they came to a clump of trees beside the road, and he turned in behind them. "We'll stop here," he said. She tried to climb out.

"Please, I am in great anxiety. I cannot delay. If it is quicker for me to walk on, I will do it." But he prevented her; and with a brutal strength that she had never before met, pulled up her thin skirts and while she struggled, ravished her. It took many minutes; he fulfilled his need, and she heard her own sick, defeated sobbing.

"Go on, get out," he said at the end, and thrust her out of the cart. She heard him drive off, and stumbled away, back on to the road whence she had come; this might happen again; for the first time in her life she was afraid.

She began to run, feeling her limbs tremble and slow her pace. Like an animal, she made her way back to the only place she knew; back to Hubertshall, away from London, away from Tom. She dared say nothing to Miss Ellen or anyone else about what had happened. She did not know what else to do except go back.

The attic was empty, with the sewing still lying there. Julia felt sick; presently she vomited thinly into a corner. Then she went to sit down in her usual place, and saw a letter. They must have put it there for her. It wasn't as dirty as the first. Perhaps it had come more quickly, or not lain about.

She was filled with fear at what it must contain. She ripped it open, and stared down at the lines. She had been right. Tom was dead. He had had an attack of massive bleeding and the parish had buried him. It would have been useless to go; she would not have been in time.

She knew what to do now. In a cupboard there were the hair trunks that the girls used for packing their clothes to take home and bring back to school when they came. Each trunk had, neatly coiled inside it, a rope for ensuring that it did not burst open on the journey, often made on a swaying coach roof. Juley opened one, took out the rope, uncoiled and measured it. It would do.

The little wood where she had met Byrne that early time was thick now with summer leaf, and the nests were empty in the boles of the trees. She took a little time to choose her branch, then found it; not far from the log on which she had sat sobbing when Tom came, and comforted her. She liked to think that he was waiting now; she felt his presence near her, and it gave her courage.

She found the branch, strong and silver, jutting out at an angle from the rest. She had to take a little time to work out how to tie the rope so that it would slip and tighten round her neck, but in the end she managed it. It was possible to climb a little way on the thick trunk, then propel herself away once the rope was certain to grow taut. She did this, and swung for a time, jerking, then was still, the thin folds of her black dress hanging, her feet pointing downwards, wearing Miss Ellen's shoes.

It was unfortunate for the school authorities that the two girls who walked down, in a day or two, to the wood were possessed of influential parents. One was the daughter of a baronet, the other of an orchestral patron known to royalty. They went, in the sentimental fashion of the day, with their arms about one another's waists, their summer muslins having been meticulously ironed by the school maids. As it was sunny weather and they were still in the grounds, they were permitted to go outside without bonnets, and their glossy hair, done in the latest fashion of a knot on top and a looped plait on either cheek, resembled the Queen's. They talked of unimportant things, brothers in the army, prospects for the holidays; then one said to the other that there was an odd smell coming from the wood.

"Perhaps it's a rabbit that has died in a trap," the other girl said. "Traps are dreadfully cruel. Papa won't permit any on his estates, but of course the poachers use them all the same. Let's go and look." They went in among the trees.

"It's — " said the patron's daughter, and gave a loud scream. She went on screaming and screaming until a teacher who happened to be up at the plots came down, to see what the trouble was; one had to be careful with young girls. Shown the cause, her eyes bolted out of her head; she gasped, and almost forgot her authority; but she remembered to shepherd the two pupils up the hill, turning them over to Miss Ellen, whose task it was to smooth over difficulties, but never before of this kind.

Hanged! And, worst of all, a newspaper reporter called, having heard of the scandal, and ferreted out the information that the dead sewing-maid had in fact been the younger sister of one of the headmistresses. At a time of year when there was very little news, this received headlines; and before many days had passed Christian and Ellen had a flood of letters from parents to say that they would not be returning their daughters to Hubertshall.

2

JAMES VOLLAND was not in the best of tempers. During his first visit home for several weeks, he had had occasion to be displeased with Maud, whose manner verged on the impertinent. It was true that Maud meant nothing to him, had never attracted him, and had borne only daughters; but she was an appanage, and should treat him with proper reverence. When he said something of the kind to her, her reply was even further out of place; its independence reminded him of her younger sister Ellen, whom he had always thanked God he had never married instead.

"You wouldn't be able to do any of this, set yourself up in London, maintain the house here, if it wasn't for the money I brought you from Papa."

There was no reply except to walk out of the room, which James did, and went to the nursery, where Jenny's dark-haired son, James Henry, was crawling about the floor. His nurse, a girl who had come as a vagrant, and whom they had at first hesitated to employ, but who had proved very good with the child, watched him constantly. James watched him also for a few minutes, aware of dissatisfaction.

Anna Belinda had come up behind her father. She was growing into a great ungainly girl, and he had no strong interest in her. His other interest meantime, in the boy, was growing muted; he could not get it out of his head that this might not be his own son.

As if she had known what he was thinking, Anna Belinda spoke up. "A woman came," she said, "and told us James Henry is Uncle Hew's son, not yours." She gazed up at her seldom-met-with Papa without fear; he was unfamiliar to her, and in any case she had only repeated what another grown-up person had said. But he rounded on her.

"What did you say? Who was the woman?"

"A fat woman. She came with Nigel who works in the kitchen. I think she is his mother."

James stared at the baby. He was Hew's

very self; his nose, which would grow into the remembered hawk's beak; the colour of his eyes, his dark hair, his very ways; confident, already depending on no one else. Why should he himself be put to the expense of rearing and educating Hew's son? Fortunately the adoption proceedings were not yet made final. Anger rose in him, then was replaced by prudence.

He would send the boy to an orphanage, he decided. It would mean a considerable saving in money. Vollands, his London establishment and Hubertshall were costing as much as they earned.

It was then that the carriage, with Ellen and Christian in it, arrived to tell him the news from Hubertshall. Christian looked as if she had aged twenty years. Ellen looked as usual.

They buried poor Julia not in the graveyard, which had been consecrated, but out beyond it in the long grass. A stone raised later bore only her name, and the date on which she had died.

A few days after the burial, Anna took a seizure. No one could tell whether it was a result of the news about Juley or not.

She was found lying on the ground, with the smell of stale blood in the room. She could no longer speak or use her arm and leg on the right side. There were to be no more admiring visits from Mr Handley; when he heard the news at first, he sent flowers.

James looked askance at Ellen and Christian; Octavia was not present, having given birth to a healthy son in course of the year. "It is as well the school is finished with," James said. "Hubertshall will have to be sold. It is necessary in any case for one of you to be here, to help with Mama; and the other can tutor my daughters."

They stared at him hopelessly. They knew that what he said was true. It would be impossible to find other situations.

A little while later Mark Volland, out by himself on the grass cleaning and greasing Buckland's old gun, was discontented in spite of the fine summer day. There had been poor Juley's burial, with its attendant disgrace; a fellow didn't want that kind of thing to be talked about at school. It was, in any case, embarrassing at Vollands; not enough servants — that crazy Nigel in the kitchen wasn't much help — and only women, except when James came home; and Mark had no illusions about James. One couldn't invite other fellows to stay, one way and another; and it was difficult to accept invitations unless they were likely to be returned. Once every holiday there would be a visit to Uncle Bart and Aunt Octavia at Surtees Hall, and certainly that was the kind of place a fellow might be proud to show off to his friends; but it had never been suggested that they be brought there, and Mark had the strong feeling that Uncle Bart, who had continued to pay his fees for Rugby, felt that he had done his duty, as he probably had, especially now that there was little Paul. One way and another, it was time to look out for oneself. Uncle Bart had promised Oxford, which would put one in the way of several openings afterwards; Mark had decided that the Church would do. It was a safe living, one met the right people, and there were prospects of advancement. One might become an archdeacon later, perhaps a bishop.

Mark gazed down the muzzle of the gun. He had made as good a job as he might of cleaning it. Nobody had touched it since Buckland went away to the army to die. It had hung on the wall of the gun-room, rusty and decaying like many things at Vollands, all these years: now it was fit to use again. He might go out rabbit-shooting tomorrow morning. It would take him out of the house, away from poor Mama, twisted and silent; and Maud, ugly and idle; and Christian, with her heart broken; and James, counting the pennies. It would be a relief to be rid, for an hour or two, of James. He watched every mouthful one ate.

James meantime was briefly occupied with the matter of the orphanage. It was an enlightened one, of the kind that no longer turned out little boys as chimney-sweeps or mill-workers at nine years old. James had made a generous donation, which should enhance his name locally despite the unfortunate scandal which attached itself to the recent closure of Hubertshall. The baby boy they were asked to take, the child of a servant girl who had got herself into trouble, would be accepted without demur. The orphanage did not, however, collect children; they had to be brought. The young nurse had, accordingly, been instructed to make the journey in the Vollands carriage, which would set her down afterwards in that part of the countryside from which she had first come, as her services would no longer be required. She set out at last with the baby wrapped in a shawl, sleeping soundly with the rocking of the springs.

Thyrza Heron belonged to a tribe as old as history, which had been noble in the days of Flodden Field. That part of the Border lands was her homeland, as it was that of the scores of men and women who slept by the southern roadsides, lit fires there, gave birth there, and sought work as they might before they died there. They had in common a bright dark eye, an air of freedom, and the proud awareness of their clan; no Heron would ever betray another. Thyrza knew this well enough when, halfway towards where they were going, she called on the coachman to stop.

"I have to get out," she said. "I'm going into the bushes."

The man, who was the same who had helped James ravish Jenny, cast a leery eye round to where she sat, but had too much sense of his own safety to try to lay hands on a Heron woman; she had nails like claws.

"Don't you be long, then," he said.

"I'll be as long as I need."

She vanished into the scrub, taking the baby with her. He waited, while the late summer night grew dark and a moon rose, and Thyrza did not return. The more he thought of it, the more he knew that he should have foreseen that she would not. It wasn't his affair; he need say nothing to the master, unless he was asked, when he'd say he had left Thyrza at the orphanage door and seen her go in, and waited, but she hadn't come back. Nobody would ask any more about a tinker woman.

Thyrza hurried on, with the warmth of James Henry held against her, till she came to a place where, between the thorn bushes, she could see the glow of a fire. She went towards it, and called out.

"It's me, Thyrza Heron."

An old woman, her face lined and brown with living out of doors, looked up. "Come away, Thyrza," she said. "There's stew in the pot."

"I could do with that. So could he. He was weaned last month." She pulled aside the shawl to reveal James Henry, awake now, his eyes aware and bright.

"That's a fine one," said the old woman. "Is he yourn?"

"No."

"Help yourself to stew, then. The men brought home a rabbit and a hare. They'll be back later."

Thyrza took stew in a cup, fed James Henry and then herself; then asked if she might sleep with them tonight. "You never know," she said. "His father's a mean man; may come looking for him."

"He'll not look here. Ay, stay."

They slept on the heath, the men in one place, the women in another. Next day, in the mysterious way these folk have, the news was flashed from the south to the Pennines to Skiddaw to Scotland, that

Thyrza Heron had a baby boy with her that was not her own, and wanted him hidden.

"They'll never find him," said the old woman, and she spoke the truth.

Part Three

1

JAMES VOLLAND at forty-seven was not a prepossessing sight. The constant pursing of his mouth had become a habit, causing a pouching of the flesh of the lower part of his face, concealed somewhat by the side-whiskers which had lately become the fashion. His hair was grey, and had thinned over the forehead; beneath the bald flesh the eyes looked out, pale, angry, and resentful of a world James was convinced had used him ill.

He was by no means a poor man, but had long ago persuaded himself that he could not afford to be generous with anyone. This had been evident in the case of Mark, whom James had tried, as soon as the boy left Rugby, to put to work in a solicitor's office; if Tillotson should die, he had told himself, he, James, would be left with the responsibility for the Oxford fees. But he had reckoned without Mark, who set his jaw and marched down to Surtees

Hall, relating the whole tale and his own ambitions, and somehow persuading Octavia's husband to continue to pay up. At Oxford, Mark had obtained a good degree in classics and history, and was now in holy orders in a living near High Wycombe. Tillotson could congratulate himself on his generosity; but he was rich enough not to be inconvenienced by it, and moreover Octavia had made him as happy as she had promised to do. They had two sons, Paul and Timothy, both intelligent, handsome, and dutiful. The family seldom left Surtees except, as was happening today, to visit Anna.

Anna was no longer beautiful, no longer witty, for her face was lopsided and she could not speak. She lay huddled on the day-bed they had had brought down, as otherwise someone would have had to sit upstairs with her constantly. When they all left her she would tap on the floor with her good hand, with a stick; and Ellen and Maud, who looked after her day and night, had come to dread the sound of it. It meant, in short, that Anna, who was incontinent, needed her sheets changed; and together they would tighten their lips and heave the sheets from below the helpless body, treating the bedsores from which Anna suffered with ointment the doctor had prescribed, but which did little good. It seemed as if the old woman would live for ever; most people who had suffered a seizure died very soon after. Anna was indestructible, and her eyes, once so magnificent and compelling, had for a long time been sullen like those of a caged animal. Their colour had faded; so had her glorious hair; there seemed nothing left of what she had been, except what was pitiful.

Christian was in the room, seated beside James's four daughters, with whom she had been saddled over the years since the closing of her school. Their tow-coloured heads were bent over embroidery, for Christian always gave them tasks to do although they were by now well beyond schoolroom age; she herself was occupied with woolwork, as in the old days; a new blanket for Mama, who no longer used afghans. Christian's face had grown lined, withered and sharpened; like James's, her hair was grey. It was hard to tell, except for the facial bones, that she had ever been beautiful. She had in fact nothing to live for, and had no affection for her charges; except for Anna Belinda, they were not interesting, and Anna Belinda, no longer a child, was too strident to be lovable.

Anna Belinda herself was ill at ease. She had been told today to put on her best gown, and, when Papa's visitors came, to bring wine into the study. There was no reason, she thought, why Nigel should not have brought it, except perhaps that Papa was ashamed of Nigel's slobbering, slant-eyed appearance. It was a sign of failure that they should have to employ such a servant. Anna Belinda lowered her eyelids, not to be seen staring at Papa, making one of his rare visits from London; but she knew his every thought, and had done so ever since he sent away the baby James Henry long ago. Nobody ever visited the orphanage, or enquired as to the progress of James Henry nowadays. One supposed he was doing well enough, or news would have been sent that he was not. Anna Belinda's mind could contemplate such situations without squeamishness. All her life she had kept her thoughts to herself, because there was nobody with whom to share them; certainly not Mama.

Maud had shrunk over the years. She sat now with a piece of knitting, aware that she would not be invited to meet her husband's visitors when they came. He was ashamed of her, as he was of Nigel; perhaps of them all. There seemed no prospect of getting the girls married; they never went anywhere. Maud did not look up from her knitting at Maudie, Beatrice and Adela, sitting at their tasks. Their heads had been stuffed with Latin by Christian, but it did them no good; they had nothing to say in company, and no looks to recommend them. Maud had only one cause for triumph, and her red-rimmed eyes gleamed with it still; the son towards whose coming James had looked forward so avidly, and at first greeted so proudly, had not been his. If she herself had had the tact to die, James would have married again, no doubt, and got a son of his own; but she hadn't died, she had lived on. She hoped to outlive James, though there was otherwise nothing in life to make it worth while. But one did not, like poor Juley, end it for that reason.

The sound of carriage wheels could be heard beyond the door, and James excused himself and went to admit the visitors, taking them round by the separate way to his study. Octavia Tillotson rose, bridling a little. She had grown into a small stout rosy-cheeked matron, and her husband adored her. He rose also, tall and white-haired by now; but he was less spinsterish than he had been in the days when Juley jilted him; happiness had improved his looks.

"We will say goodbye, Mama," said Octavia, and bent to kiss the flaccid cheek. The two boys followed obediently. If James would not introduce his friends to them, they would not stay; and being Tillotsons could make the fact evident.

"Come soon again," said Ellen, who had been silent till now. She looked much the same as she had always done. She and Maud saw them out, and were rewarded by the sight of a strange and magnificent equipage, which must have cost a great deal of money; sleek and well cared for, like the liveried coachman who waited by the horses, talking to the footman who had stood up behind. The Tillotsons entered their separate carriage and drove off; it was handsome enough, but nothing to compare with that other. James was up to something. "I am thankful," announced Octavia, "that we are as we are, dependent on nobody."

Tillotson looked at her fondly. Dear little Ocky would come out with odd statements from time to time. As far as he was concerned she might say anything she chose. He could have searched the world and never found a better wife. The wound of Juley's forsaking of him had healed long ago; it had been a mercy, in the end; her own, poor girl, had been deplorable.

"You had best take the wine through now," said Maud.

Anna Belinda rose and went out, her blonde head high. She'd known perfectly well when to fetch the wine; there had been no need for Mama to tell her, seated there watching everything, as always, with her red eyes. It would be pleasant to get away from being watched and ordered, but there didn't seem any prospect of it, either for herself or any of the girls; it was like living through the whole of one's life at school, not that any of them had been allowed to go there. They might have made friends there, met other people. As it was —

Nigel had left the tray ready and polished in the kitchen. He was good with silver, rubbing and rubbing with a happy smile on his face until the silver shone like the day. Annie and George Volland, neither of whom had married and who stayed up at Hubertshall to keep it aired and dusted, couldn't touch Nigel for silver. All George did was scythe the grass, and get drunk.

She fetched the wine — Nigel was not permitted to touch it and the glasses, set them out on the tray, and marched towards the study. On the way she remembered she hadn't smoothed her skirts; the new crinolines got crumpled if one had been sitting down in them. Otherwise, she looked not too bad; she never took much heed to her appearance, it wasn't worth it. Papa, when he was here, never failed to tell her how unattractive she was; it was as if he had a grudge against her for that time about the baby, and for being a girl at all.

She opened the study door, bringing up her knee to steady the glasses. As a result, she made an ungainly entry. There were two men sitting with Papa, both of them young; at least, she supposed the hunchback was young. The other was the most glorious she had ever seen. He had dark, crisply curling hair, brown eyes set at a slight slant, a straight nose, and an elegant figure. He rose politely, and so did the other; Anna Belinda heard James's satisfied drawl.

"This is my eldest daughter. My dear, this is Lewis Crozier and his brother Julius. They have agreed to purchase Hubertshall."

Anna Belinda was aware of the brief sweep of the brown eyes over her, assessing her; of course she had no chance with such a beau. Avidly, the hunchback watched her also; she disliked the sensation that his glance gave her. However he could not help his deformity, or the fact that he had bad teeth, a hook nose, and large strong hands. He himself was quite small. They all sat down after Lewis Crozier, ever courteous, had drawn up a chair for Anna Belinda. From time to time she noticed his glance upon her, summing her up, but not as though it affected him. She was aware of a trembling throughout her whole body that she had never known before. How courteous he was! It was evident that he came from the great world, one she herself had never seen. He would know London very well. He would have been to Court.

The talk did not include her, nor was she offered wine. Lewis Crozier would have handed her one of the glasses, but James said unctuously that she did not drink it. At that, Lewis replaced his own glass on the tray and said he would not drink either. This gesture, above all the rest, won Anna Belinda's heart. After the brothers had gone James told his daughter to remain. "Sit down," he said. Anna Belinda did so, a trifle bewildered that her father should still desire her company. His pale eyes watched her; he was smiling.

"Lewis Crozier is a very handsome young man, is he not? I observed that you could not keep your eyes from him."

She flushed, and said nothing. "It would

be a waste of your time to think of Lewis," James told her. "He is married to an heiress, whose money has enabled him to make an offer for Hubertshall. He intends to turn it into a shooting-lodge for the new weekend parties which the Prince of Wales has made fashionable since his marriage. Lewis will stock the grounds with birds, and make the house fit to entertain the highest in the land, with whom he is, naturally, already acquainted."

She hardly heard him after the first shock of blood to her heart. Of course, she should have known that Lewis Crozier was married. She managed to keep her face expressionless, her eyes down.

"The reason why I sent for you," James continued, "was in order that you might be seen by your bridegroom. Julius Crozier has already agreed to marry you."

"That hunchback!" Despite everything she could not keep the terror from her voice. To marry *that*! Like most girls she was not clear what full marriage meant; it was the more remote at Vollands in that the house was peopled mainly by women, with her father seldom at home. But she knew that children were born of a marriage, though not how; and the thought of having a child to Julius Crozier was one of horror.

"You are fortunate," James told her drily. "In your position, without looks or any great fortune, although naturally you are my heiress, it might have been very difficult to find a husband for you. You would then have been compelled to live out your life like your aunts Christian and Ellen, old maids both; as it is, in your new position I hope that you will be able to marry off your sisters suitably. Lewis, you must understand, needs a hostess for the Hubertshall venture; and I have said that you will be capable of filling the position. What you do not know you will soon learn; you have a reasonably quick mind, and can copy others."

She clenched her hands together. "I will not marry that hunchback. You cannot make me. Why cannot Lewis Crozier's wife be his hostess?"

"If you will not marry Julius of your free consent, you will be beaten into it. Lewis's wife is not in good health; another person is necessary."

Anna Belinda knew more about beatings

than before: over the years Aunts Christian and Ellen had whipped her diligently, oftener than the rest because she had a will of her own, which they said must be broken. Had she any of that will left? She heard herself say, in a firm voice,

"I will go to Aunt Ocky. You cannot touch me there."

"You are wrong," said James smoothly. "I have legal rights over you, and can obtain you back again from wherever you may go. I do not advise you to make an issue of this matter; if Julius were to hear that you are unwilling, or for that matter Lewis himself, the sale of Hubertshall might fall through: but I can assure you that if that happened, you would feel the weight of my anger to a degree you have never yet envisaged."

He stretched out a hand suddenly. "Come, let us leave it till tomorrow," he said with the charm he could still summon when he chose. "Lewis has invited us both — yes, yourself as well — to go up and view the suggested improvements he intends to make to Hubertshall. You will have the opportunity of talking with both brothers, and it may be that you will find Julius less obnoxious than you now think. His deformity is, after all, not his fault."

She bit her lip, but knew that she would go. She would go to walk with Lewis across the scythed grass, feel his arm under her hand, hear his voice, golden as honey, flow on as it had done in this very room. And if she went to live at Hubertshall, she would see him every day.

James's pursed mouth relaxed. The difficulty of selling Hubertshall had been minimised when he had stated to Lewis Crozier that he had a daughter who would make a wife for Julius; hitherto no woman would look at the younger brother, not only by reason of his hump, but because of his nature. Anna Belinda would not find that out, however, until, as they said, the knot was tied. James was pleased with his own handling of the situation.

He had lately purchased a new phaeton in London, and took advantage of the good weather to drive down to Vollands in it; also, as Anna Belinda suspected, to show it off to his fine new acquaintances. He handed her into it, and they drove off. The Crozier brothers were, he informed her, staying with the Yesters at Hanfield. This was meant to impress Anna Belinda, who knew the grand Yesters only by means of a slight nodding acquaintance at church; gone were the days when old Lady Yester had invited all the Volland daughters over in Pippa's time. The Vollands had, in fact, sunk long ago into obscurity; Maud would have made a vapid hostess, and a houseful of women, old and young, were not a social asset, especially when one considered Anna's paralysis. So the phaeton bowled on hopefully, with the intention of altering the situation as soon as it might be done. Anna Belinda downed her misery, and made herself enjoy the drive and the prospect of seeing Lewis Crozier again.

He was waiting for them, smiling and handsome in the sunshine. He wore a pearl-grey suit of clothes that had obviously come from a superlative tailor. He bowed to Anna Belinda and tucked her hand in his arm, leaving Julius to walk behind with her father. Lewis might have been waiting for her alone, and during the walk round Hubertshall she allowed herself to think that this was indeed so, and that they were everything to one another. He showed her what had been the dormitories, long fallen into neglect; Annie and George had grown old and were no longer able to keep everything as it should be. "We will have to find new servants," he said. It was as though he were the husband, she the wife, going over their future home together. Behind them, the other two talked in low voices. Bedrooms would be built here, Lewis informed them, with doors opening into one another. He did not explain why.

The ship on the central tower had blackened long ago, its gilding corroded with the years. "Why a ship?" asked Lewis idly. "We are nowhere near the sea."

She told him about great-great-uncle Hubert, and how he had once briefly been a sailor; and the other things about him, and made Lewis laugh. His laughter was sharp and brief, not hearty; it was as though, having found a point he appreciated, he stored it away in his mind and was thereafter finished with it. But the brown eyes surveyed Anna Belinda with approval. "That is exactly the kind of thing our guests will like to hear," he said, and she realised that it was assumed she was coming. A coldness came over her; what would happen if she said outright, 'I am not coming here. I will not be your hostess. I will not marry your brother'?

But she had not the courage; the moments were too precious, and after all she was going to see a great deal more of Lewis. Where was his wife?

They went over the grounds, where Lewis intended to fashion an artificial lake stocked with waterfowl, and landscaping to the front. The other slopes would be used for coverts, and he was anxious to grow heather for grouse, "But it is difficult, and may not be a success. We might have to content ourselves with pheasant and partridge, perhaps snipe from the marshes; but guests for a weekend will not want to walk far. If it rains they will play billiards; you saw the room."

It was all arranged for. She herself was so. She felt increasingly that she was caught in a net, from which there was no escape; and that the one who controlled it was Lewis. There was a ruthless quality about him, a determination to succeed in whatever he undertook; but he fascinated her; she would never be free of him. She knew that she would agree to the marriage.

Anna Belinda Volland and Julius Crozier were married in September in a quiet ceremony at Vollands, with few guests. Mark, having come from High Wycombe, officiated. The bride wore a gown of oyster-coloured faille, and her sisters were the attendants. Present were the Yesters, the Tillotsons, the bride's immediate family, and Lewis Crozier and his wife. It was the first time Maria Crozier had been seen by anyone here, and at sight of her it was realised why. She was stumpy, with thick features, and in an advanced state of pregnancy; a shawl of Richelieu lace, which would have made any other woman look beautiful, was flung over her shoulders to hide her state. Lewis was the bridesman, and left her alone. Anna Belinda did not look at her groom while the vows were pronounced. When he put the ring on her finger, her hand was as cold as ice.

Cake and wine were handed round, then the guests left out of consideration for Anna, who had watched the ceremony from her day-bed. She seemed to be trying to say something, but what it might have been was never known. The evening passed somehow, then it was time for the bride to go upstairs and be undressed; the wedding night was to take place at Vollands, then the couple would drive to Hubertshall next day.

The master bed had been kept aired and turned by servants and the family since the days when Jenny had endured James's transports in its depths; it was dry and comfortable. Anna Belinda, unlaced from her oyster faille, received the only instruction she was ever to have from her mother. Maud stood with her red eyes surveying her daughter, and said in a low voice, "Whatever happens, do not make a disturbance; do your duty."

Anna Belinda climbed into the bed, and being tired, fell asleep. She did not understand what her mother had meant;

no doubt it was one of those morally uplifting remarks to which Maud gave voice from time to time. The feather mattress was deep and warm, and nothing disturbed her until, late in the night, she was awakened by a man's hand crawling across her stomach.

What happened next filled her with horror and disgust. She had never imagined it. She knew however that she must endure it; this was marriage. She felt his weight panting above her and was thankful that she could not see him. His breath was foul; she must endure that also. He used her all night, and in course of it a cold pride came to her; she would never, never let anyone know how she felt, her revulsion, the pain, her loathing of the things he did to her, things she had never known or dreamt of. If this was to be her life, she must live it. There would be compensations. There would be Lewis Crozier. Lewis must have known that this would happen. He was heartless in such ways. She knew that already; and still loved him. He had married that ugly little woman for her money, and still — still — still —

The mattress jogged creditably. It was near morning. Presently he left her and turned over on his side to sleep, and snored. He had not addressed a word to her, nor she to him.

Next day she had herself dressed in silence. She would keep this silence all her life. If anyone thought to mock her, they would be disappointed. She knew now what her future would be. There were no more surprises.

2

THERE was a spate of deaths at Vollands after that. First of all went Nigel Evans; innocent, cheerful, obedient Nigel, as near the perfect servant as anyone could want. He developed a cough in his chest and shortly his breathing changed: Ellen, who was among the few to take any notice of him, sent him to bed. Thereafter she nursed him as well as she could, but he grew no better. When he was blue in the face, she sent for the doctor. He gazed down at the patient and nodded.

"Most of them go sooner in this way," he said. "He is fortunate to have lived so long, and happy enough."

"We will miss him," said Ellen. The doctor looked at her with some concern; she herself had a bad colour.

"Have you nursed him alone?" he asked, and Ellen said she had. "The rest have enough to do with Mrs Anna," she told him. Christian had in fact refused to do any more lifting, and Maud, who helped nobody at any time, had insisted that it was improper for her daughters to nurse a man, a servant. So it had been left to Ellen.

"Will you allow me to examine you?" the doctor asked her, and when he had done so he said, "Your heart is not in a state to permit further lifting of bedridden patients. You must take care of yourself. I will tell Mrs Volland."

Maud showed no emotion at the news, but Ellen, for the first time in her life, began to pamper herself; and would lie on a chaise-longue in the way Anna had used to do, repeating in a kind of litany that she was not to be allowed any heavy lifting. Meantime Nigel died quietly, and was buried. As if he had done both at the most convenient moment for everyone, George and Annie Volland were sent down the hill; Lewis Crozier wanted younger servants. The old pair stood at the door of Vollands helplessly, and it was impossible not to take them in. Annie could cook, at least, and George could make himself useful about the grounds; all he asked was his habitual evening off on Fridays, when he went and got drunk. Once Beatrice, crossing the grass, met him on his way home in summer, and he handled her in a way to which she was not accustomed. She screamed, and George was forbidden to show himself inside the house again. Otherwise things continued as they had been, until Jim the tinker came.

He was tall, with fine shoulders. He might have been about twenty years of age, but men of his kind looked older than they were. He had a great hawk's nose on him, dark eyes bright as a bird's, a skin burnt brown with the weather, and a shock of black hair roughly cut. His bearing was that of a prince.

It was Maudie who came to the door. Seeing his tattered coat, she looked him up and down in a patronising manner. "If you want money," she said, "there is none here for you. Take yourself off."

"I want work, not money. I heard you need a gardener." His eyes looked through her; she was skinny, plain and out of her twenties, and her manner angered him. Maudie hesitated; she was not accustomed to make decisions. "You had best come and see my mother," she said. Maud was in the drawing-room with Anna; it was better not to call her to the door.

He followed her, the dark bright eyes surveying everything in the house. All this by rights should be his, according to Thyrza before she died. He would have it, one way or the other; or else know why.

Maudie did not remember any of her uncles, and was not prepared for the drama that greeted the tinker's appearance before Anna. The old woman had been lying as usual with her head to one side for ease; now she turned it, and her glance, piercing and amazed, fastened on the tinker's face. Anna thumped her stick once, then let it drop; and raising her arm, pointing with her sound hand, slowly spoke, as she had not done for years.

"Hew."

The sound breathed through the room like a bird's call, like the last note of a song; then the arm fell flat on the covers again, the eyes still left open, glazing fast. She was dead. Maud, who had said and done nothing, began to scream. The tinker waited. Perhaps, when they had done with their fuss, they'd remember him. Folk died every day, but his own people took it quietly.

Anna's funeral was the excuse for taking Jim the tinker into employment. They could explain to James that it was necessary to pay another man to help scythe the grass across to the graveyard, as George would not manage it in time. "Get rid of George, then," James would say; he was averse to the spending of any extra money, and if the old man did not earn his keep, he could go. It would then be further explained that Annie, now almost blind but still a good cook, would undoubtedly go too, and they would obtain no one else as cheaply. In the end James would grumble, agree, and let the matter rest.

The day dawned fine, and Anna's coffin was followed to its place by a number of carriages, some full, some empty but sent as a sign of respect. The Yesters had sent theirs, and the people who had bought Clarefountains from old

Squire Fielding. Handley, Anna's one-time admirer, sat alone in his; he was still a bachelor, white-haired and solitary since his mother's death. The Tillotsons came, and the Crozier brothers, leaving Anna Belinda in the house with the other women; Maria Crozier was too near her time to attend. It made an impressive little procession towards the place where the sandstone vault reared among the lesser graves. At the iron gate, holding it open, stood the tall tinker and George. After the company had emerged and walked through, and Mark Volland's voice droned on about ashes to ashes and dust to dust, Jim the tinker stood looking at a certain grave. It was Jenny Volland's.

He knew Jenny was his mother. He had gleaned all he could from Thyrza, and still more from old George, who had had certain things in his turn from the coachman, long dead. Jim knew how James Volland had deflowered his mother in the coach, going round the long way among the trees. He knew — it had been noted, after all — how she had been forced to receive visits from James in her own bed, then later brought down to his, always against her will. "She never liked him," George had said. "She never wanted it, but she had to do as she was bid." The only thing Jim was not told, for nobody knew, was that he was Hew's son, not James's. Hadn't he been called James Henry, after his father? And that father had abandoned him as a baby, after stating that he would adopt him; had meant to put him in an orphanage, except that Thyrza had run off with him and they had never been found.

Jim hated James Volland, accordingly, with a hatred that was as strong as acid, as enduring as stone. He would take his vengeance in his own way. Those girls — hardly girls by now, any of them, and not a comely one among them — were his half-sisters, and even among tinker folk it was incest to sleep with a sister. He, he would dishonour them every one, in time. He would make James Volland ashamed to show his face in the grand places he frequented. Somehow, after it was all done, he would acquire his inheritance. He swore it to Jenny's bones, lying under the earth.

The burial was over; Anna's body was stowed beside Henry's, her husband so long dead. Tinker Jim stood at the gate, his face impassive. He saw James Volland go past, and the pale glance travel over him. In fact James was thinking that the young fellow was standing correctly, had cut the grass creditably, and would do well enough to take the place of George, who could not last long.

As a married woman, it was considered in order for Anna Belinda to be present in the birth-chamber at Hubertshall when Maria, Lewis's wife, had her baby. In fact Anna Belinda felt at a loss; she had no idea what would happen, or how babies were born. She had made a success of her duties as hostess, and the grand folk who came already to Hubertshall to shoot were appreciative of her cold impersonal manner and witty tongue; the latter had developed since leaving Vollands; she had not known she possessed it. She was able to supervise the cooks and chambermaids, tell them what to do in no uncertain terms, and make herself feared and respected. That her nights were full of horror, that Julius furtively, insistently, took his rights without stint, no one would have suspected; her icy manner concealed both her loathing of her husband and any other feelings she might have. With Lewis it was different; but Lewis had lately hurt her in an unexpected fashion.

She turned her head towards where Maria's dumpy form lay on the bed; grunting sounds had begun to come from her. Anna Belinda asked if she could fetch her anything; lemonade, tea? But the labouring woman wanted nothing. There were after all servants about the fire, heating water. They would see to whatever was needed, in whatever way. Her own ignorance need not be exposed.

She thought of Lewis again. She must accustom herself to the fact that he had a mistress, who was very beautiful, with sea-green eyes and fashionable clothes, and who had been installed in the comfortable lower floor while poor Maria occupied the upper one. Constance Hetherwick had arrived as soon as the last coat of gilding was put on the tower ship; Lewis must have kept her in London for some time. It was understandable, of course, with Maria being as she was; and Anna Belinda knew that she herself was not beautiful, had no attraction but her wits. Lewis sometimes enjoyed those, and she had made up her mind always to entertain him, never to weary him, never to expose her woes, to ensure that he still came to her, as he did daily.

"Ugh," said Maria from the bed. She soon began to howl regularly. The women clustered around and presently the child was born; a puny boy. There had been small difficulty, but Anna Belinda was appalled at what she had seen; so that was how it happened, that was how — and why — husbands did what they did in bed. A certain thought appalled her; she prayed that she might never, never have a baby by Julius, probably a creature with a humped back. If it happened, if she knew for certain it was going to happen, she believed that she would want to kill herself before the birth.

The chain of death at Vollands captured George, who was found dead in his corner of the local taproom. He had been used to sit there during long silences, and it was thought that this was one more; then suddenly the barmaid screamed, and the dead man was borne away in due course to his coffin, and buried in the graveyard. The tinker watched as he had done before, silently, from the gate.

Old Annie was inconsolable; they had been the only two of Hubert Volland's bastards left, and now she was alone. By degrees Tinker Jim insinuated himself into her kitchen, and helped the half-blind old woman with tasks she could hardly find the heart to perform any longer. Also, from time to time he brought her fresh fish from the stream, where he had set lines; they used to fry them for breakfast.

The fishing-tackle, and more than that, came from George's outhouses, where he had never allowed anyone but himself to go. There was in addition, thick with dust, an earthenware still, and although Jim could not be troubled to make whisky he used the great retort to brew herbs, of which he knew a good deal. The resulting beer was strong, and he could vary it as he chose; the brewing did not take much time. He would carry out his tasks in the house and grounds and then vanish, for hours at a time, into the outhouses. What he did while he waited there nobody knew, and Jim kept his own counsel.

Beatrice, the middle sister, prided herself on her curiosity; Aunt Christian, who had educated all of them, had impressed upon them the need for the cultivation of enquiring minds. Beatrice was neither thin nor fat, was plain like the rest, and owing to her mother's sad inheritance had false teeth early. That summer she spent a good deal of time out of doors, and could not forbear to notice that Tinker Jim spend a good deal of time out of sight.

She ventured, accordingly, to put her head round the door of the near outhouses where one entered; as children they had never been permitted to go in, and Beatrice felt a forbidden thrill as she surveyed the dusty sunlight, and piled and cluttered objects she could not name; otherwise there was an old churn, a sieve that rust had rendered useless, a dairymaid's stool, other such things. She could not at first see anything of Jim, but hearing her footsteps he appeared through the further doorway. She thought he might be uncivil at being undisturbed, but he looked perfectly calm; he was naked to the waist, as it was a summer's day, and his eyes surveyed her with a look she found strangely exciting.

"What is it?" he said, and Beatrice bridled.

"I can come in here if I choose," she told him. "This house is my father's. What do you do in here?"

"What I please. Come in if you will." There was a pleasant, aromatic smell coming from the further part beyond the dividing wall. "What is that?" she asked. "What are you making?"

"Come and try it, if you like. It's herby beer."

Beatrice felt very daring. She had never drunk beer; a lady didn't. But it would be something to tell the other two; or perhaps after all she would keep it to herself, she wasn't sure which. She followed Tinker Jim into the further room, where the still bubbled; she had never seen anything like it before. "Try it," he said, and poured out a cupful; Beatrice drank it, and it tasted strange, but not unpleasant.

Afterwards, after she had gone away, Beatrice found herself with strange feelings, almost dreams; above all, she thought of Jim with his body naked to the waist, and how it was different from a woman's.

Jim meantime concocted a fresh brew with pennyroyal in it, which made a woman want a man. There was a bed of pennyroyal in the vicarage garden, and he knew his way through the hedge. She'd be back. This was the first of them; the others would come slowly, he was not yet sure how; but they would come.

Maud had long ago lost interest in life. It did not occur to her to speculate why nobody except her mother had ever loved her. She had thought that, once free from Anna and the constant lifting and changing, soaking and drying of sheets for the sick woman, she would be free; and so she was, but freedom brought no joy. Her daughters had never meant anything to her; they had been reared by Christian. Christian now spent her time in her room, reading, occasionally coming downstairs to pry and open doors suddenly, as if to remind one that she, and not oneself, was the daughter of Anna Volland. As for Ellen, who might have been company to her own half-sister, she fancied herself as an invalid, whether or not she was one, and lay about all day as Mrs Anna had done. James seldom came home and, when he did, looked over the household accounts, carped, and then departed. Maud knew that it was not surprising that he never noticed her: she seldom noticed herself these days; ill-fitting dentures, thin grey hair, a shapeless corseted figure, and feet twisted with bunions. Also — and Maud knew it — there was a little comfort these days in the way of a glass, every so often, of whisky or brandy. Who could blame her? It made life bearable, if only just.

It was true that she was proud of Anna Belinda. The venture at Hubertshall had been such a success that only last week Albert Edward, Prince of Wales, had come down with a shooting-party, leaving his beautiful Danish Princess behind, as she was expecting a child as usual. What lives women led! Maud remembered her own travails in the early years, and shuddered;

and all for nothing. Nevertheless Anna Belinda was doing well.

As if her thoughts had crystallised into reality, a carriage drew up at the door, and Anna Belinda herself got out, dressed fashionably. She has come, thought Maud, to tell me about the Prince's visit; thoughtful of her. She rose from her place, and stood ready to greet her daughter.

It was evident from the beginning, however, that Anna Belinda had not come to exchange pleasant news. For one thing she looked sallow; the mustard-coloured velvet hat she wore did not become her. Maud suspected the truth at once; but one avoided speaking of such things unless it became necessary.

"Will you take a little marsala?" she enquired, and realised that between the whisky and her dentures, her speech was slurred. Anna Belinda declined coldly, sat down and spread her skirts. Mama was reeking of whisky; one should have known.

"I believe that I am going to have a child," she said. "How does one tell? I have no one to ask except yourself."

Maud informed her, prudishly but with enough certainty to make the facts clear. So it was true; and the exhaustion after the Prince's visit, with all the preparation that had gone before, and the degrading sickness that came daily, were witnesses to the truth. Perhaps she would die; women did die in childbirth; even she knew that. It was no longer necessary to think of killing oneself.

"When will it be?" she asked. Maud elicited a few questions, then told her that also, as far as possible. "And I shall be there with you, my dear child, of course," she added. "It is not so far away."

As far as the stars and moon, my mother; you will be nowhere near me, if I can help it.

She rose shortly, pleading duties at Hubertshall, and left in the carriage.

She was walking with Lewis later that afternoon among the parterres which they had caused to be made on the site of the girls' gardens in old days. There was little sign now that Hubertshall had ever been a school. The heather slopes Lewis had hoped for would not be a success, though he had sent for growers from Scotland; there was some mysterious factor about heather, not yet fully understood, and without it there could be no grouse, for the young lived solely on the shoots. Nevertheless the Prince and his party had enjoyed themselves well enough, and had promised to return.

Anna Belinda did as she had resolved to do, and told Lewis that she was expecting his brother's child. He turned a pleased face to her; whatever reticence a gently bred woman should display in speaking of such a subject to a man was not expected by him. He and Anna Belinda knew one another well by now, he told himself; but was disenchanted by her next remark.

"Lewis, I have a thing to ask. Julius will not leave me alone. He has not done so since our marriage. For the time, until the child is born, can you ensure that I am left in peace? He will listen to you, but to no other."

So that is the way of it, Lewis Crozier thought. For too many years his brother had been starved of women; now, he glutted himself of his wife. Lewis frowned; he was not used to be left at a loss. "Endure it for tonight," he said presently, "and by tomorrow I will have a solution."

It would not do, he knew, to lose so valuable an asset as Anna Belinda had proved herself to be about Hubertshall. When she had gone in, he took himself to one person he knew would be able to think of a practical answer; Constance Hetherwick. Constance, her green eyes glinting, produced the answer at once; an exquisite little negro page got from London, in bright satin tunic and turban, looking as if he had been left over from a previous century. She invited Julius to her apartments for wine, and left the boy with him.

That night, for the first time since her marriage, Anna Belinda slept alone. She did not ask herself where Julius might be, nor trouble when, in the ensuing days, she saw him trail about after the little negro, and make him presents. She was too thankful for the freedom from thrall of her own body, in which there would now grow steadily, from week to week, Julius' child. Lewis was careful, of course; when guests came to Hubertshall the negro and Julius had to be separated or hidden. Certain things, even in the rapidly expanding social climate encouraged by the Prince and Princess of Wales, were still not acceptable.

It took three visits to drink pennyroyal beer before Jim had his way with Beatrice, almost without her knowledge of it.

She had thought constantly of him. It took a few days for her to summon the audacity to go back to the outhouses when she knew he was there. He did not touch her; he knew that if he were to place a hand on her knee, or finger her arm, she would rise and go; and he had no intention of letting her go until he was done with her. Then, the third time, he saw that she was ready; she was holding her breasts, and making moaning sounds; she had downed a full noggin of beer.

He laid her back, and pulled up her skirts readily; her drawers defeated him, but only for moments. Her head turned from side to side, uneasily, as he entered her; he was quick about the business, knowing that once he was within her he could use her at his pleasure. This took place, and her moans changed from sounds of need to sounds of ecstasy; he thrust on, aware that she would not forget the experience, whatever else she forgot. In due course he left her, rose, and went out. When she came to, he thought, she could dress herself, and either come back again if she chose, or stay away. He had had one of the daughters; he had promised himself four. The beer wouldn't work for all of them; he must think of something else.

Beatrice came back. Although she was hardly conscious of what had happened to her, the awareness was pleasant; as pleasant as anything that had ever happened in her life.

She began to go to Jim in the outhouse often, and it didn't matter soon whether there was beer or not. She began to expect, and revel in, her moanings; it no longer mattered that Jim was only the gardener, only a tinker; he had that which brought her wild joy, deep contentment, a delirium of love. She would wait all day in the expectation of it, and when it was cold or raining would be in an agony of disappointment. But, one day, the sun shone again; and she went to him, and pulled up her skirts and took down her own drawers, so much hurry was she in. They began to couple; and before Beatrice could start to pant and moan, there came an anguished cry from the door.

"Beatrice! How dare you! How — " Then a gurgle; and before Beatrice could cover her naked thighs she had seen what had happened, and who it was; Aunt Christian, and she was lying on the ground, dead. She was the one whose heart was supposed to be all right, but it couldn't have been.

After Christian's funeral they decided that the outhouse was no longer safe. "Come to my room," said Beatrice. "You can climb up the apple tree, straight into the window. We all sleep on that side. We'll have to be a bit quieter, that's all."

"It's not me that makes the noise," he said. But he climbed up the apple tree nightly, and came to her in bed; and she tried to stifle her cries so that Adela, who slept next door, and Maudie, who slept inside the door after that, would hear nothing; and thought she was successful.

She was not. Jim was tying the lines in the stream that ran through the coppice, having set the caught fsh aside, when Adela came upon him. He could not tell whether she had come of set purpose, or merely by chance. She was the most attractive of the sisters, not only by reason of being the youngest, and in spite of having to wear spectacles with metal rims for short-sightedness. She peered now at the fish, lying dead beside the bank; he had hit them on the head with a stone.

"What do you do with those?" she asked.

"Have 'em for breakfast."

"You don't ever give us any. This is Papa's estate, and they're his fish."

"Those who want fish, catch 'em." He was not sure after all that he liked her any better than the rest; she had the same uppity manners. Papa's estate, indeed! One day —

Adela sat down beside him on the bank. "I suppose you don't have to give us anything you don't want to," she observed, adding, "What is it you do to Beatrice at night? I hear her, and I hear you. I know it's you, because there aren't any other men at Vollands."

So she heard them, did she? He suddenly bared white teeth in an animal grin. "You don't want me to tell you what we do," he said. Adela pouted a little; he had noticed that her teeth were her own.

"I do want you to tell me. Beatrice won't. She says I'm not to tell anyone. She treats me like a child. They all do. Please tell me. I won't pass it on to a soul."

He noticed that she spoke like more of a child than she was; possibly the result of being the spoilt baby of the family for many years. He was determined by now to have her, probably today; it was an opportunity. The thing was to tease her, get her to do anything to find out what she wanted to know and what he wanted to show her.

"You'd yell," he said. "It hurts a bit at first. Afterwards it's all right."

"Beatrice likes it. I can tell from the sounds she makes."

"Well, you'll make the sounds, if you let me show you without yelling."

"I won't yell, I promise. I promise."

"Lie down, then. Lie on your back."

She had, in fact, remained quiet; biting her lips at first, for she was made narrowly and he had to force his way up. He found out, having once disarranged her clothes, that she had knock knees. Once the pain was past she began, like Beatrice, to pant, and presently he made sure that the sounds came. He lay with her for a long time, knowing there was no prying aunt to come; in any case, they would hear footsteps making their way across to the coppice. The coppice reassured Jim in some way; he felt no harm could come to him there.

He withdrew from Adela at last, and presently, having tidied herself, she said in a small voice, "I know now. Will you come to me in my room after you've been with Beatrice in hers? I'm next door."

Thereafter Jim the tinker worked harder by night than he did by day, for there was nobody now to supervise him in the garden. On the other hand, after he had nightly climbed the apple tree, both sisters welcomed him so assiduously in turn that, although he was a young man of dedicated energies, he would depart, at last, in the early morning, weary; ready to sleep in the stables, where his quarters were, much longer than any employer would have allowed him to do; and James Volland came down sometimes. Had James slept in the house on his visits there would, of course, have been no question of the apple tree on those particular nights; but James had developed the habit of putting up at Hubertshall, where he might hope to meet important company.

Beatrice, therefore, and Adela continued to enjoy their nightly pleasure. It was natural that Beatrice, at the beginning, should have been jealous that the younger sister should be visited as well; but she had to put up with it, for Jim told her roundly that it was both or none. He himself found it convenient to go on to visit Adela's room, for he could walk from there straight to a window that looked out from the half-stairs, and gave on to the roof of the stables, thus cutting out a cold roundabout journey when one had been lying in a warm bed; that is, two warm beds.

One night when he had been coming to them for several weeks, and it was getting near winter, there was a full moon risen. It shone high in the sky like sixpence, silver and round. He was with Beatrice, and getting ready to go. She wrapped her legs round him, to keep him with her, and clung to him; he saw her pallid plait of hair fall back in the moonlight against the pillow. Her teeth were out, steeping in a basin on the commode.

"Don't go yet, please, just once more. Don't leave me yet. Please."

"Tomorrow," he told her, freed himself and went out of the door. Beatrice was left clawing the pillows with envy of Adela; she was certain Jim stayed with Adela longer than he stayed with her.

She was right. Jim preferred Adela, albeit coolly; apart from her knees, she hadn't a bad body. He slipped into her bed and pulled her nightgown up to reveal it, lying curved and hollowed in the light of the moon. He began to fondle her breasts; she started to whisper, fearful of Maudie overhearing next door, that Anna Belinda had had a son. Mama had been in the drawing-room with Aunt Ellen when the news came from Hubertshall, and had sent for them at once.

"That's because she's married, of course, Anna Belinda, I mean," she told him. "One can't have a baby unless one is married."

He smiled to himself; both sisters, if they only knew it, had had more than one chance of that. It still amazed him to discover how ignorant of ordinary life these no longer very young spinsters were; of course, the poor bitches had hardly known a man, except their father.

He finished, and let himself out beyond the door, beginning to put on his coat for it was cold. He had it halfway on when he saw Maudie, whom he could not stomach, at her open door. He had had no idea how he could fulfil his oath to himself and take her, and had left it to whatever powers looked after him to find a way. Now, he waited. She began to speak, horrified.

"I saw you coming out of my sister's

room. What business had you in there?"

He slid out of his coat and flung it over her head, silencing her. He carried her back to her own bed, flung her down on it, and, sprawling across it and over her, relieved her of her virginity. It only took a matter of moments. Afterwards he whipped the coat from round her head, leaped to the passage window, opened it, and was gone through it before Maudie could sit up. At the same time he was laughing to himself, laughing at the completion of a vow mostly performed. They could say what they liked to one another, those three; or nothing. He himself was off. It was safer not to be at Vollands for a while. He would go to Hubertshall, and find out there if they needed a beater for the coming season. It was near enough to Vollands, yet far enough away to be in another world. The bright moon lit him on his way up the hill. Of them all, Maudie was the only one to have a baby. When it was known, with the disgraceful circumstances, and Mama and Aunt Ellen had had their hysterics, it was decided that of course James must be told; best in person, not in writing: such

248

things never looked well in writing. They must wait till he came home.

Maudie herself went about in a state of dreary shame; nobody would believe that she hadn't encouraged that tinker. As the months passed, the changes in her body became obvious for all to see; some babies sat back and some forward, and this one kept well forward; she couldn't show herself in church or anywhere else. Papa, when he came home, would be furious. That was the worst part of all.

3

ANNA BELINDA was so happy with her son that the world could have stopped turning without its troubling her. From the time when they had told her, "It's a beautiful boy, with fair hair," she had loved him. He was a Volland. There was no sign of any hump on his back; he was as straight as an arrow, with a strong body and muscles that showed like a swimmer's. He would be a handsome man. He was the whole of her existence. Lewis came to see him and was pleased; she was glad of that; Julius came, and was proud of himself for having fathered a son. She could not even loathe Julius any longer; let him go to his little black boy. She, Anna Belinda, for the first time in her life, was fulfilled. She wanted to call the boy Hubert, after the founder of the house: and this was permitted.

James was inspecting the household accounts at Vollands when his wife and

Ellen came and stood before his desk. He glanced up in irritation; he had an appointment shortly at Hubertshall with the director of a rival bank, and was looking forward to pitting his wits against the other's over a glass of excellent brandy. The sight that greeted him was in any case not inclined to make him stay; Maud had grown careless in her dress, and Ellen was a bony-faced old fright nowadays, leaning on a stick.

"What is it?" he said testily. There was a silence; Maud was terrified of breaking the news that must be broken. Ellen stepped in.

"If you will not tell him I must do so, Maud," she said. "James, one of your daughters is expecting a child by the gardener. He has, needless to say, left. I understand he is at Hubertshall as a beater. You had perhaps best see him for yourself."

James's face expressed rage and incredulity. He ignored Ellen and rounded on his wife.

"How could you let this happen? You have been neglecting your duties. Which of the girls is it?"

"Maudie," she whispered, trembling. James's eyes protruded.

"Maudie? She is the one I would have thought had the most common sense of any, not that that says much. I will see her. Send her to me at once."

The snivelling Maudie was brought, palpably pregnant. "When did this happen?" demanded James in a voice of ice.

Maudie knew when it had happened. She assured him it had only happened once. She would have gone on to tell her father that both her sisters were as bad if not worse, only he would not listen to anything she had to say. He stormed at her, " Is this man married? Do you know that, or not? Did it occur to you to ask?"

"I could not ask, Papa. I had no opportunity. He — "

"Do not answer me," said James unreasonably. "If he is not married already, then he must marry you. I shall speak to him at Hubertshall today."

Maudie screamed, and began to have hysterics worthy of her mother and Ellen; how could she marry a common man, a workman, a tinker? "You should have thought of that before," James told her callously. "You have risked my position in society, and your own; now you must pay the price."

She could have told him that he had never provided her with any position; never given her or her sisters a season, pretty dresses, an opportunity of meeting young men of their own kind; he had left them to grow into old maids alone, without diversion, without friends. But she dared not say it; instead she was bundled out of the study door and fled weeping to her room, where neither Beatrice nor Adela came to console her; they had been strictly instructed to stay away. As for Maud, when James had gone she poured herself a glass of brandy, with a little water. It was not of the superior variety James would drink presently at Hubertshall, having had to be insinuated into the accounts as soap and candles: but it was a comfort.

Anna Belinda walked behind the baby-carriage, which was being propelled by a nursemaid in streamers; otherwise she could not have kept her own hands in her muff, and it was a cold day. Young Hubert did not appear, wrapped warmly as he was, to trouble about the cold. His cheeks were a healthy pink, and he slept through the journey, yawning and laughing now and again to himself in his sleep. She could not stop watching him; her days were spent in adoring him, playing with him, cuddling and feeding him. Already his hair was forming guinea-gold curls, and his eyes were as blue as the sea.

Anna Belinda herself was as nearly beautiful as she would ever be in her life; happiness had given her a certain radiance, her clothes became her, and the success with which she managed Hubertshall had given her poise. It was true that Lewis might soon begin to complain of the time she spent with the baby. He himself, she could retort, spent all of his with his mistress. Constance had obtained such a hold over him as the months went by that unless visitors were at Hubertshall he was seldom to be encountered outside her apartments. His own little son, also named Lewis, was neglected, and seemed backward. As for Maria, her husband left her alone. Partners here did not match; Anna Belinda glanced without interest at the stretch of winter grass near the new lake, not cold enough to be frozen over except in the transparent skimmings of ice that bewildered the waterfowl. Julius was down there, throwing a ball for the negro boy to catch. Their laughter reached her; she shrugged a little, and walked on.

The path wound past some bushes which had been planted now for a year, and screened the bare parterres where the new beater, who also helped in the garden, was tidying dead plants and turning over the earth. To her surprise Anna Belinda heard her father's voice; he should have been closeted with a Mr Van Hoyt, a banker, who had come down especially to meet him. She almost went to remind him of it, then realised that his voice was raised in anger. He could be talking to nobody but the young beater. Anna Belinda signalled to the nursemaid to make her own way ahead with the baby-carriage, and herself stood still to listen; it was perhaps not very creditable to eavesdrop, but Papa could be unpleasant, particularly to classless persons such as workmen. If she might help in the matter, she would.

" — and having ruined my daughter's reputation in this way, you must marry her."

Tinker Jim gave a short laugh. "Why should I marry an old woman? We've never exchanged a civil word. In any case, *sir*" — he laid emphasis on the title with triumph — "it wouldn't be within the law, you see. A man can't marry his half-sister. I'm your own son, if you want to know; my name's James Henry Volland."

Anna Belinda heard her father give a snorting sound; she feared a seizure. But James began to speak again, almost smugly. "There you are wrong, my good fellow," he said. "If you are indeed James Henry Volland — and I have no proof of it — then you are my brother Hew's son, not mine."

"You know that? Can you prove it, as we're talking of proof? I'd sooner be his son than yours. I'll marry Maudie, that being the case; do we stay at Vollands, or not?"

"Vollands will be left at my death to my eldest daughter, Mrs Crozier," replied James coldly. "All that concerns me at present is my second daughter's right to a wedding ring."

"I'll buy her a ring, then," said Jim.

"Then that is settled; let it be as soon as possible," said James coldly, and walked away.

Anna Belinda trod across the dug earth, away from the clustered bushes. "Listen to me," she said to the tall young man, who had resumed his digging. "I heard that. I heard all of it. It was I, as a child, who told my father you were not his son. I can remember my uncle Hew; he was a soldier, a hussar. You are very like him. As a baby you were not like my father. I suppose I thought I was clever; perhaps I was trying to attract his notice to myself. He had staked everything on this son, you see; your mother was a Volland girl, Jenny; you know that."

"Ay. I know that from Thyrza." He was leaning on his spade, the dark eyes staring at her.

"Thyrza rescued you from the orphanage, where my father would have put you. I owe you something for all of this. While I live, you shall stay at Vollands, with your wife. Nobody will cast you out, I swear it."

"Then I'll do aught I can for you," he told her, and again, "I'll do aught I can."

The only clergyman to preside at so deplorable a wedding was of necessity the Reverend Mark Volland. Mark, who had risen in importance as the years went on, and was assistant to the Suffragan, was not too pleased to have to be present on so questionable an occasion; moreover, his housekeeper had recently died and he wanted to interview possible successors. However, as it was a family matter he came; made Jim and Maudie man and wife, then walked round greeting such members of the family as were present. James, naturally, had given away his daughter; her two sisters, eyes downcast as if they had never known the groom, followed the bride, who was well disguised in lace. The groomsman, a fellow-beater, knew his place and troubled nobody. Anna Belinda was there, proudly carrying Hubert, who was much admired, but whose presence could not fail to make everyone think, though of course it must remain unmentioned, of that other baby which, from the look of the new Mrs Volland, would appear very shortly indeed.

Octavia Tillotson had declined to be present. She was a widow now, and could please herself; not that, in fact, she had ever done anything else. Maud looked her worst in a bodice front of soiled coffee-coloured lace, with her hair attempting to stay in curl, and failing. Ellen stumped about on her stick, indicating even in silence that the whole business was disgraceful. She found a kindred spirit; the eminent clergyman Mark had become was horrified at the social decay evident among the Vollands. "Mama would have had half these people out of the house, and would never have permitted this wedding at all," he murmured, and Ellen nodded vigorously. He had sympathy for her; she was, as he put it to himself, a cut above the rest: a former headmistress was a person one might know. He waylaid her midway across the worn carpet: told her of his difficulty about finding a housekeeper; and before he left had arranged that she, and none other, should come to fill the place. Ellen forgot that she was a semi-invalid; it would be a relief to get away from Vollands, into civilised society and among predictable people.

With Ellen gone, Maud was left to her own devices; and these took the form of keeping an eye on her two youngest daughters. She moved into the upstairs room which Maudie had formerly occupied, banned the room with the window looking on to the apple tree, and made Beatrice and Adela share the middle one; when they were in bed she would lock them in. Often in the morning she would forget to unlock the door, and the two would beat and scream till they were heard and released; as far as amorous adventures were concerned, these were in any case at an end.

"I didn't know," said Adela, when it was first found out, "that he'd been with Maudie as well."

Beatrice, who had not known either, preserved her counsel. Henceforth she

260

would be the elder sister, who kept the younger in control. "In any case it's very wicked, and look what it leads to," she told Adela. "We are finished with it, both of us. It is best forgotten."

Adela supposed that, as Beatrice said, they were finished with it. In fact, the memoried nights stayed with her for the rest of her life. At first she would writhe with desire that it might happen again, despite everything and everyone. But gradually Beatrice's stronger will prevailed; as the years went on, the pair of sisters turned into dim, repressed creatures who might never have lifted a petticoat or dreamed of a man. They continued to share a room; it was more proper. As for Maudie, she had had no intention of allowing the tinker to touch her again. The indignity that had been done to her made her very mind bristle; when her new-made husband addressed her she replied as she always had, in a haughty manner, like a mistress to a servant. Tinker Jim acted as the men of his tribe would do in such a case, if it occurred; he took off his coat, got hold of a broom, and gave his bride a sound beating. After that Maudie was no longer haughty. Within herself, like Anna Belinda, she developed pride; and showed her black-and-blue shoulders and back to nobody. She kept her pride even amid the agonies of childbirth; the child was a boy. Suckling him Maudie found degrading, and worse still the discovery, before he was weaned, that a second child was on the way. If she had foreseen her future, she might have quailed; got with child yearly, left alone each summer, when Jim went off to his own people, taking his fill of younger women there among the spinneys and moors; then in autumn, when it began to be cold, he would come back to Vollands, watch the new birth, start another baby, and be off again in spring.

He never touched the women upstairs again. A locked door alone would not have kept him out. Maudie sufficed him.

One day in March it was balmy weather, almost like early summer. Crocuses had been planted the previous autumn in the grounds of Hubertshall, and showed their yellow, white, and purple heads agreeably.

Hubert had learned long ago to walk, and his mother decided to take him to look at the flowers; it was the middle of the week and there were no visitors. She dressed him herself in his new blue coat and nankeen trousers, and set a cap on his curls; and herself put on a wool cape suitable for walking.

They set out, the little boy holding Anna Belinda's hand, and were unaware of what was proceeding in the nearby suite of rooms Julius kept for himself and Sammy, the negro. Sammy was naked, running about and laughing, his teeth flashing white in his ebony face, his graceful limbs smooth as rosewood. Julius called him, longing to feel their smoothness and grace: to caress the boy gave him the greatest pleasure in life, and he could not by now do without him for long. But Sammy was capricious today, and would not come; he wanted something, and Julius in a fever promised him anything he might like to have: a brooch, new slippers, oil for his hair.

"No. No. I do not want any of these. I want — "

"Tell me what you want, and you shall

have it, I promise." The great hands reached out for the boy's rounded flesh; but still Sammy eluded their grip.

"You will not do it. You will never do what I want. You would be afraid."

"I promise, I promise — " Julius was almost crying, the saliva dribbling from his thick lips. "Whatever you say to me I will do. Only come to me."

"Afterwards. I will come afterwards. First you must do as I say."

He writhed, like a boy in a Greek dance of fertility. "I want very much, very much indeed to go in the boat on the lake. You must row it. We will go to the island. There I will let you touch me." He began to laugh. The boat on the lake was new, and he was aware that Julius was afraid of water. He enjoyed teasing him in such ways, asserting his own power. He saw the hunchback's face blanch now almost to grey, his mouth fall open.

"I cannot row. I have never done it."

"Then we cannot make love."

Sammy swaggered away, his buttocks swaying rhythmically. "I will dress," he announced. Julius suddenly wailed and gave in. "We will go down, then," he said. Someone would surely see them if there was trouble. He was aware that Lewis did not like his openly associating with the dark boy before visitors. But for once, with none about, it should cause no comment; only, he himself was trembling with fear. His hunched shoulder would not allow an even pull at the oars, he was certain; but it was after all not far to the island from the boathouse.

The island had been made of mud and driftwood, with trees planted to hold it together; it was intended as a place for the birds to nest and multiply. It looked, from the bank where the boathouse stood, further away than Julius had anticipated. He climbed carefully into the boat, feeling it sway dangerously beneath him. Sammy sat in the bows, his bright turban like an ensign. They thrust out into the lake. Julius managed clumsily to control the oars. The waterfowl dived and glided out of their way, being not yet used to this advancing monster.

All went well until Julius lost an oar. He gave an exclamation; he could not lean over to that side without losing his balance and probably upsetting the boat. He called out to Sammy, who showed the whites of his eyes and did nothing. They drifted aimlessly, going nowhere near the island, the oar floating further and further out of reach. Julius tried, with the one that was left, to pursue it, and shortly thought he had done so; leaned over, raked for one oar with the other, and was promptly in the water. He sank, rose, struggled and shouted; the boat had capsized, and he could see Sammy's turban floating; neither of them could swim. The only thing to do was go on shouting in the hope that somebody would hear. But the lake was deeper than Julius had supposed; his cries and struggles were soon submerged in muddy water.

Anna Belinda both saw and heard them. She was with Hubert in the little wood that had been planted at the top of the rise. She had told him that he must not pick the crocuses, but he was a spirited and disobedient child and needed constant watching to ensure that he did as she said. She would never whip him;

whip that pearly flesh, so free of moles and marks! It would be desecration; but Hubert was certainly naughty. However he turned to her, forgetting the flowers for the time.

"Men in boat," he said, then, "Boat in water."

It was at that moment she saw them. She knew Julius from his shape. Hubert would not know his father from here: they hardly met. She saw the boat capsize, knew that she should run down for help; and stood still. "They have gone for a swim," she told Hubert. "Let us go and look at the rest of the flowers."

She prayed that no help of any sort would come; an icy strength sustained her mind. Later she heard that the two bodies had been found near evening, the boat, the oars, the turban floating not far off. She and Hubert had taken the other path back to the house in the end, so that they would see and know nothing. Once they had reached their rooms she filled Hubert's mind with other things so that he would not remember the men who had gone for a swim.

Nobody foresaw that Lewis Crozier would be grief-stricken at the loss of Julius; there had never been any open affection between them. But, after all, they were brothers, and near of an age; and Julius' deformity had no doubt made Lewis protective of him. At any rate, he wept at the funeral of the drowned man: and thereafter vanished to Constance's apartments, leaving the conduct of affairs, and the entire reception and care of guests, to Anna Belinda.

She was beginning to grow wise in the ways of the world, in particular a world which, as was the fashion nowadays, permitted husbands to come here without their wives, and wives without their husbands; fully making use of the double-entry rooms which Lewis had designed and which had puzzled her at first. Now, a list would be given her as to who would be placed next to whom; a marchioness with a duke, a pretty new arrival with A. E. himself, who returned frequently. The Princess of Wales never came, but her fashions did; she had begun to wear tweeds, and these were copied by all the ladies who went out for a picnic luncheon after the guns had done their early work. It was Anna Belinda's task to oversee these luncheons, with their cold grouse, sent from Scotland, and champagne on ice from the well; the hampers would be loaded and conveyed to the chosen spot, with the ladies' elaborate hats, decorated with birds' feathers, converging over the feast at last laid out on snowy cloths. Then they would return to the house, change for tea, then change again for dinner. It all took time, and Anna Belinda saw very little of her son.

Lewis emerged at the end of about ten days, having had such food as he would eat sent in to Constance's rooms. His face was puffy with drinking and his mouth sullen. He set off to see that everything in the house was as it should be, and as he made no complaints Anna Belinda assumed that this was so; but she would have liked a word of praise. However she was not the worst off of anyone. Poor Maria, whom Lewis by custom ignored, was ill with misery; she had lost weight, and although she sat at table with Anna Belinda in their dining-room as usual, she ate hardly at all.

Another had suffered, though differently. Constance seldom left her apartments except to mingle with the guests, who presumably thought she was one of themselves; her exquisite clothes, paid for by Lewis out of Maria's money, would have enabled her to face the Queen if that lady had been interested in fashions. Constance had, also, a bold confident manner and much wit; she amused Lewis when he was feeling like himself. This day, however, she was not feeling like herself either; her colour was that of paper and the remarkable eyes had shadows beneath.

"Damn him, damn and triple damn him," she said of Lewis. "He promised me there would be no brats. Now I'm sick as a dog, have been all week. Would you do me a favour when it's born, and say it's yours? It could be, with your husband alive till the other day. I can't have these people asking questions about me."

She looked hopefully at Anna Belinda, then the green eyes grew cunning. "After all, you owe me a favour," Constance said.

"I got the nigger boy for you, didn't I, and kept the hunchback off you? What I'm asking isn't much. I'll have the trouble, not you, and of course Lewis will pay for all of it."

Anna Belinda refused. She still had some feeling for Lewis; the thought of acknowledging his mistress's child as her own was repugnant. "Damn you, as well, then," said Constance, "and damn Maria. Nobody would believe it was hers, from the look of her; he never goes near her anyway."

"She is very ill," said Anna Belinda coldly.

Constance flounced off. She had to conceal herself during the coming months, which did not please her as she enjoyed the admiration of attracting A. E. himself on one of his visits. She never forgave Anna Belinda for not assisting her in the matter of the child. When it was born, a little girl, Lewis doted on it, and paid far more heed to it than to his own son. The child was christened Zoë; and at that same time Lewis's wife Maria died, of sorrow and neglect.

"No, I will not turn Hubert over to a governess; he is much too young. I intend teaching him myself when he needs it, until he is of an age to go to school. In any case, he and Lew do not get on; Hubert chases Lew all over the room and bullies him."

Lewis listened idly, his red-brown eyes watching her as if she had been some strange and amusing species. "You will not have time for all of that with your duties here, Anna Belinda," he told her. Seeing her stiffen, he added cunningly, "You do not know how indispensable you are to me. Nobody else could handle the guests as tactfully as you do, not to mention the kitchen staff. Without you, I would long ago have had to abandon the notion of a guest-house at Hubertshall."

"You could find another hostess," she said gruffly; but it had pleased her greatly to be flattered by him, even though she knew by now that there was bound to be a motive.

"I will not find another such hostess, but governesses are easier to come by. The one I have in mind is married to a portrait painter, a difficult fellow, but he might find patrons among the guests. She is well qualified and experienced, and said to be good with children."

"Get her for Lew, then; but leave me out of it."

"I must say this to you," he told her earnestly. "Now that my wife is dead our positions are difficult. People will ask why I live here with my brother's wife as hostess. They are quick to scent scandal in a situation where there is none. The presence of Mr and Mrs Lumley would right matters."

"Why do you not marry Constance?" she said sullenly; his overt rejection of her hurt her deeply. He smiled.

"Constance is married already, to a worthy young man who cast her off when she came away with me. There is a son, a little boy the father keeps."

"That is hard on the boy."

"Shall we bring him here, to share the governess? That would make a covey, if you like; my Lew, your Hubert, Constance's Robin, and Zoë in time."

She could tell from the way he spoke that he had set his mind on the hiring of the governess, and disliked her already; but she herself could refuse Lewis nothing. In any case, and they both knew it, he was Hubert's guardian under the boy's father's will.

It might have been easier had Gertrude Lumley been different. She was as she was, however, and by the time she had been in the room five minutes Anna Belinda had summed her up; the young woman was sly.

She was not an uncomely creature, having fine dark eyes and hair and a plump bosom. She dressed plainly in dull clothes, in the manner of her profession. Evidently she had been a governess only since she married her husband the painter, and there were unspoken implications that Gertrude's background before that had been more distinguished than her present mode of life led one to assume.

Peter Lumley was either a genius or a madman, it was not yet evident which. He was given to wild bouts of temper which led his wife to keep him out of the children's way. He also, as Anna Belinda noted early, drank a good deal. No doubt

Gertrude's salary helped to support him and to pay for his tippling. Later it was discovered that the Lumleys had in fact been bankrupt and that all their possessions, including Peter's easel, had been distrained. Anna Belinda took this information to Lewis in the hope that he would get rid of the couple from Hubertshall; but he looked at her with the expression of languid amusement he sometimes used, and said nothing.

Constance at first doted on Gertrude, who was always willing to take charge of the baby, leaving its mother free to move with elegance among the house-guests. These were beginning to include many persons of distinction; the Prince of Wales had not come this year, but there was among others an eccentric duke who was a fine shot, a Privy Councillor, two well-known clubmen and a baronet. The ladies who flocked about them all had not diminished in number, but they were outshone on every occasion by Constance, wearing, in the evening, a set of silver filigree earrings, bracelet and necklace Lewis had given her at the time of Zoë's birth. During the day, her piled hair supported hats the fantasy of which were unequalled by the efforts of any other lady; and her wit made the parties go. Anna Belinda found herself increasingly in the position of bookkeeper, caterer, and housekeeper; sometimes she did not appear among a particular party of guests at all. Again, Lewis was aware of it, and did nothing.

Peter Lumley had a mild success with quick portraits, especially in pastel. A room had been set aside for him to receive his sitters, and Anna Belinda saw to it that it did not reek of whisky when they came. It was one of the minor tasks that the arrival of the Lumleys had put upon her, rather than relieving her of anything at all except the custody of Hubert. He adored the new governess, who seemed to have a way with children; even poor little Lew was brighter when Gertrude was present.

"What did you learn today?" Anna Belinda would ask her son at the end of it. He was so beautiful that it tugged at her heart. He smiled, showing well-spaced milk teeth.

"A was an archer who shot at a frog,"

he said. "There was a picture of the archer, in a hat."

"Did Lew learn about the archer, as well?"

"Don't know. Lew doesn't learn much." He lay down on the floor and began to turn somersaults, an accomplishment he had perfected some time since. Anna Belinda tried to down her jealousy of the woman who enjoyed Hubert's company all day. Parents gave their children to governesses and tutors as a rule, she knew; but Hubert was all she had; the hours passed dully without him. That such beauty, such agreeable mischief and instant wit, should have been conceived in the terrible night hours with Julius seemed almost incredible; but it had happened.

She was troubled with dreams of Julius now and again. It seemed to her that he came and lay with her, as he had used to do, treating her cruelly, perhaps in revenge for letting him be drowned. She would wake with her fists stuffed in her mouth for terror of crying aloud. With the dark he would have gone, only to return on another night. There was nobody to whom she could speak of it; not the scornful Constance, not the demure Gertrude Lumley, least of all Lewis, who after all had loved his brother and knew nothing of her share in his death. She must endure the visitation, tell herself it was only a dream, which would be gone by morning.

4

"GRANDMA says will you please send down the carriage for her? She's got something to say."

Maudie's middle two, who had walked up, were like all the rest, living images of Tinker Jim, with no trace of their mother's fairness. They had washed their faces to come, and were more or less presentable; but Anna Belinda was still glad it was the middle of the week and that there were no visitors. Her mind quailed at the thought of having old Maud up here as she was these days; but she herself could not spare the time to go down, and whatever it was about was evidently important enough for Vollands to trouble Hubertshall, which seldom happened.

She gave the two children a ride down in the carriage, much to their delight, and hoped there would be no fleas left behind. Presently it returned, containing Maud. Anna Belinda went quickly to

279

enter the carriage and sit beside her mother, to keep the old woman from entering the house; she did not want Lewis to meet her. The carriage smelt strongly of whisky, false teeth, and old age. Maud wore a hat which was battered and lopsided, a dress with stains down the front, and gloves with splits in the fingers. Her face was a ruin compounded of years, drink, disappointment and basic plainness. Her grey hair straggled thinly beneath the hat.

"What is it, Mother?" asked Anna Belinda quietly. Any other daughter of any other mother would have brought out Hubert, with pride; but Maud did not even remember to ask for her grandson. Her mouth opened and shut for moments like that of a fish, then she said, "It's James. He's taken a stroke like his mother did. Took it in bed, and not alone."

The mouth pursed and she bridled; James's sins had found him out, her expression implied. "Who is nursing him?" asked Anna Belinda. She was aware of no emotion concerning her father; the news might have been that of a stranger.

Maud looked sly, her eyes sliding obliquely beneath their red lids. "Well, I can't, as things are down there," she said. "You wouldn't believe what goes on. He's away for the summer with the two eldest, to teach them tinker ways. Maudie's expecting again. It wouldn't do to have James there, with things in that state. I wondered — we wondered, Beatie and Adela and I — if you'd take him, and look after him. He always said he'd left everything to you; it would be a sign of gratitude." She sat back.

Anna Belinda was aware that she ought to have foreseen it. It was true that the two girls, as Beatrice and Adela were still called, could have nursed their father in the remaining upstairs room; but all the children, and Maud herself, would upset any invalid, and there were the stairs to climb up and down with food and slops. At Hubertshall, on the other hand, there was plenty of room, and descendants of the Volland bastards were always at hand to do any rough work, any lifting and emptying and washing of linen. She supposed she would accept. She laid her hand, somewhat gingerly, on

Maud's soiled and splitting glove.

"I will see to it, Mother," she said. "You go back in the carriage now, and look after yourself."

Maud's mouth drooped as she was driven off and she put out her teeth on her tongue. Anna Belinda was getting so much above herself she couldn't even ask her old mother in for a cup of tea.

James Volland had been in bed in his London flat with a little shopgirl from the department store in which he had lately taken out shares. He had acquired a taste for deflowering virginities, and some trouble was taken, by those whose interest it was to please James in such ways, to see that his needs were met. Having in the present instance satisfied himself, with marked effort as the maidenhead in question was unusually tough, he felt a sudden burst inside his head; his mouth sagged, he began to babble nonsense, and his limbs lay useless on one side while still functioning on the other. The deflowered shopgirl screamed repeatedly, bringing James's manservant running; it was as difficult to cure her hysterics as to help his master; in the end, partly to relieve his own feelings, he slapped her face. After that it was a question of bundling her out of the flat before the doctor came; she wailed that she had been promised money.

"You won't get any from me, that's certain," retorted the manservant, and she fled crying down the stairs, her clothes half buttoned. The doctor's verdict was predictable; Mr Volland had had a seizure and must be looked after; had he any family?

James was, as might have been expected, a difficult invalid. From the time he came to Hubertshall he caused the maximum inconvenience possible for anyone in his semi-paralysed state to achieve. At first Anna Belinda had thought she herself, with the help of Grace Volland's eldest daughter Phoebe, might manage to deal with him and also keep him company in his room while she did the books. But it was impossible to be with James all the time, and one day Phoebe wrenched away and refused to have anything more to do with him.

"He's a dirty old man, that's what," she said, her face scarlet. "He may only have one hand that works, but he uses that, and I won't say how. I'm sorry, Mrs Crozier, but you'll have to find someone else."

It was the same with all the rest. It was the same with the trained nurse whom eventually, with great difficulty as they were not easy to obtain, she employed for what turned out to be a very short time indeed. The nurse was to stay with James by night, to let Anna Belinda have some much-needed sleep. Mistakenly, instead of Mrs Anna's stick he had been given a bell; and rang it all night long for the least thing, waking everyone with earshot. Also, the nurse's starched streamers and comprehensive blue uniform did not prevent James's treating her as he had treated all the other women who came within reach except his daughter. In the end Anna Belinda employed men to look after him and to sleep in his room; and this meant changing her own.

The new room which she assigned herself was along the passage from Peter Lumley's studio, and she could not help overhearing what went on there, particularly when he forgot to shut the door. His wife seldom visited him; when she did, they would have some short cold talk, then Gertrude would leave to resume her duties. It was evident that they no longer lived as man and wife. She continued teaching the children, and Hubert, now growing tall, remained greatly attached to her. Lew trailed behind, constantly told by everyone how stupid he was and, accordingly, becoming more so. A little confidence would have helped him, and Gertrude no doubt gave him what she could. Hubert, however, was her pride and joy, and had progressed far beyond the archer who shot at a frog when disaster struck Peter Lumley in his own studio.

The eccentric Duke of Wavertree had become a frequent visitor at weekends, not only for the shooting but for a sight of Constance, whom he adored. She held off his attentions without offending him; accordingly he thought her a chaste woman, a relation of Lewis's. One day he offered to pay Peter Lumley to take her portrait. "Beauty like yours, m'dear, ought to be set down for the future," he told her. "Wear that hat with the feather," and arranged with Peter to portray her exactly so. Peter listened idly; he was accustomed to pleasing himself, and was not going to be told how to make a portrait by any slightly daft old nobleman. He nodded and agreed, however, stating the fee, and the Duke of Wavertree went off to the butts.

Constance moved in due course across the studio, aware that she was looking her best. She wore a blue dress and matching hat, with an emerald green ostrich feather trailed across the brim. It was far enough from her eyes to enhance them, and she looked a deliberate study in blue and green. She could never resist making advances to any man, even though they were not followed by a reward; and throughout the sitting she played Peter like a fish, using her eyes and her lovely mouth, and her hands on which Lewis's aquamarine ring bore out the colour-scheme admirably; he had given it to her while he was still entranced with her, but Constance suspected that lately he had grown complacent; the notion that she could ever lose a man was however inconceivable. She would teach him a lesson, nevertheless; she would flirt with this artist, make him ravenous for her. There was, moreover, Wavertree. She smiled a little, her full lips stretching. To be a duchess! His first wife was dead. A pity there was William.

"You can move if you want to," said Peter Lumley dispassionately. "There is no need to keep perfectly still."

The portrait took four sittings, and Lumley would not let it be looked at until it was completed. When it was, Wavertree was there to see it. His big face, criss-crossed with little broken veins, showed pleased anticipation; his light-blue eyes bulged happily. Constance was with him, her hand on his arm. Lewis was not present. Peter Lumley turned the portrait round.

For a moment there was silence. On the easel sat the face of a wanton woman. In some way Peter had etched in the lines of greed, of lechery, of cruelty, arrogance and conceit. It was hard to say how it had been done; but as a rendering of Constance Hetherwick as God would see her on the Judgement Day, it was unequalled. Constance's hand tightened on the Duke's arm; but he wrenched away, roaring with anger.

"What's this? What's this? Made her look like a whore. Don't expect me to pay you a penny. Tear the damned thing up. Burn it." He walked out.

Peter Lumley began to laugh. Constance walked across and slapped his face. Then she hurried out, along the corridor, back to her own rooms. From somewhere came the wail of a child crying. It stopped suddenly, hushed by its nurse. It was Zoë.

Presently there was the sound of tramping feet; the Duke had come back. He was muttering to himself, then spoke more loudly, finally almost shouting to whoever might hear.

"Horsewhip the feller. Horsewhip him. Not a gentleman, can't challenge him. Here we go. Horsewhip him, I say."

Anna Belinda came out of her room too late to stop what happened. Wavertree had gone to the studio, a whip in his hand which he had obtained from the stables. He would have done as he said and whipped Lumley, but Peter flung himself at him, both strong hands about his throat; and squeezed. It was probable that he did not mean to kill; but the Duke was not in good health. He dropped to the floor, and rolled over, his face a grey colour. He was already dead when they came.

Hubertshall was silent. Gone were the sounds of the beaters in the long grass, the chatter of the guests, the occasional popping of the guns. There was only silence; following the brief, obscene incursion of reporters and the other curious, anxious to know why a duke had died here suddenly. His body had been taken away at the same time as Peter Lumley had been marched off between two policemen; and the distinguished company had left in a body, flocking to its carriages; anxious not to be known to have anything to do with the scandal. It was almost certain that none of them would ever return. There were other places to which to go for diversion, where one was not compromised. Old Hubert Volland's gilded ship twirled in the wind, with no one watching, then was still; like the water on the artificial lake.

Nobody knew what Lewis thought. He had strolled in, after everything was over, to examine the books with Anna Belinda as he did regularly. She was well aware that he kept an eye on every item, as James had used to do; nothing escaped him. It pleased her that he had never reproached her for her management of the accounts. James lay in his bed not far off, snoring slightly. The men she had selected handled him efficiently and saw to his comfort. The bell rang less often now in the night.

They were together in companionable silence when Constance walked in. She was in travelling dress, a tweed cape and a hat embellished with gulls' feathers. Her maid followed her with a valise, then went on outside.

"I am going," Constance said, as if it had been of no moment. "I am returning to William. He will be surprised, don't you think? But after all it is some time since you have been any kind of lover. I have endured enough of it, and I shall endure no more."

Lewis stared at her, and suddenly she launched into a vituperative attack so fierce that it might have been thought that he had done her an injury. Anna Belinda listened, horrified, wondering if she ought to absent herself; but Lewis laid his hand on her arm and made her stay. He still said nothing.

"You realise that I am going, then? You understand that I will not come back? Why should I, to this godforsaken place which will soon be derelict, to which nobody will ever come again? When you brought me here, it was different; you were full of promises then."

"Have you taken your jewels?" Lewis asked her politely. The green eyes flashed.

"Naturally I have taken them. I have given you payment in kind, have I not?"

"But you have left your child behind."

"Zoë? She is *your* child. I didn't ask to have her. You may keep her with my blessing, for what that's worth."

"Then go," he told her. She stared for a moment, as if unwilling to believe that her departure could cause so slight a commotion; then snorted unbecomingly and flounced out. Presently they heard her carriage drive away.

Anna Belinda looked at the man she loved. It was best to say nothing at all. Only in such a way could she comfort him.

Worse befell. Hubert, who was allowed to visit his mother after dinner, told her that Lew had been seedy all day. "He wouldn't do any work, and Mrs Lumley was cross at first, then she said he was ill, and he began to be sick and have a headache, and she put him to bed. He's there now." Hubert's bright eyes registered interest in the fact of illness; there was his grandfather, and now this.

Anna Belinda was frantic with anxiety lest he catch whatever it might be Lew had caught. She kept him with her next day, and herself went to see the governess. To her surprise, Gertrude Lumley was attired in an apron, pouring cold water over Lew's head while he sat naked in a bath by the bedside. The child was restless and flushed.

"It is to keep the temperature down," Gertrude told her. "You were wise to keep Hubert with you today. I was about to send a message to tell you to do so when he did not come."

Anna Belinda felt resentment; who did the governess think she was? "I hope that young Lewis will progress," she said coldly. " If I can do anything to assist you, pray inform me."

"It is much better for you to keep away from the sickroom, and keep Hubert away also."

As that suited her well enough, Anna Belinda did not reply. She went back to Hubert, who was gleeful at being allowed off lessons; and sent him out riding on his pony, which he had acquired in the previous year after a smaller one had been sold. She put on a coat and went out to watch his shapely erect body in the saddle; how proud she was of him! How she prayed that he might not catch this fever! He must grow to be a man; anything else would break her heart.

Hubert did not catch the fever. Shut away from everyone but Gertrude Lumley, Lew grew worse, with the expected stomach rash and pea-soup stools and delirium; the latter, overheard by none but the governess, revealed what an unhappy little boy Lew had been; but it no longer mattered. He improved, and was well enough in a day or two to receive a visit from his father, of whom he was terrified. Then he sank; and by the end of the week was dead. Gertrude rose from her task of nursing and minding, took off her apron, and went to her room to fall sound asleep. Others washed the body of the child whom nobody had loved, put it into its coffin, and closed the lid. Lewis had come once, looked down at the remains of his son, gone away and sent notices to the papers. Nobody knew what he felt, or if he felt anything.

Anna Belinda heard the news with mixed feelings. In her opinion little Lew had been mentally backward and would never have made a fit heir for his father. Nevertheless she was sad at the death and knew that Lewis, for all his outward calm, could not have remained unmoved. Her own feelings overcame her; she had loved Lewis for years; had she no right to comfort him, to say a word to him in his bereavement? She had kept silent at the other deaths, the disasters; surely now she might speak?

It was late in the evening. She had dressed for dinner as she always did, even when, as was usually the case, no one was there to see. Her dress was of silk and made a hushing noise as she found her way along the passages. There was a light under Lewis's door. Anna Belinda did not knock; she was risking everything by this visit; either he would welcome her, or else would reject her. She steeled herself against the latter; after all, she was used to it, but now —

She turned the handle of the door, silently. The lamp was lit beside Lewis's bed. In the bed were two people, a man and a woman. The woman lying in his arms was Gertrude Lumley. The pair were murmuring together like lovers. They had not heard her come.

She went out. She did not remember closing the door, going back down the passages, gaining her own room. Once there, she gave way to floods of weeping. It was as though all the tears she had wanted to shed in her life were shed now. She wept into the small hours of the morning, silently, in order to waken no one, though she could have given way to an ugly sobbing. When she looked in her glass at first light she saw a plain woman with red eyes. As before, her pride came to her; no one should ever know, should ever suspect, that she had wept all night, that she had loved for years, that the man she loved preferred other women at any cost. At least — and this was better, far better, than nothing — at least she had his occasional company.

5

JAMES VOLLAND took two years to die. He outlived his daughter Maudie by seven months. The latest bout of childbearing, resulting in twins, killed her. Anna Belinda could not leave her father to be present at the funeral, but heard that immediately after it the tinker family, including the babies who were looked after by the eldest girl, and a black nanny-goat that fed them, made their way north for the summer pilgrimage, except that in this instance nobody was left behind. There were, of course, old Maud and the girls, living in their own upper part of the house from which they hardly ever came down. Anna Belinda saw to it that James's payments to them continued; they did not starve. Their state was described in telling terms by Mark Volland, who had conducted the funeral and who had recently been made an archdeacon, as he had hoped in his youth.

"The way they live is deplorable. Your mother is drunk most of the day, forgets to eat or to cook; often they live on raw eggs. I could hardly believe it when I saw the state they were in, unkempt, almost ragged, and — I must say it — not too clean. Something ought to be done about them." He looked meaningfully, from beneath eyebrows that had grown shaggy and white, at Anna Belinda. She shook her head, whose hair had turned grey.

"I cannot undertake any more, Uncle Mark. I pay, or rather my father pays, for a servant to look after them; clean the grates, light the fires, bring in food and so on. I have enough tasks here to occupy more than one person; the running of Hubertshall — "

"Hubertshall is sadly, since the recent scandal, empty of guests."

She smiled a little, and he thought how worn her face had grown; she had never been a pretty woman, and now would be noticed by nobody. "We have hopes that soon, Hubertshall will regain its former popularity," she replied. "I can tell you this is confidence; we have had a letter from Marlborough House signifying that the Prince of Wales would like to spend a weekend here in the autumn. If he comes, others will."

"That is true," said Mark, impressed. "What do you think induced this renewed interest? It is some time since the unfortunate business occurred, but it will not have been forgotten."

"That is partly it; time has glossed over the notoriety; also, he heard of poor little Lew's death, and sent informally to convey his regrets. He has a kind heart, and will help those in misfortune where he can; he is not entirely bent on pleasure. I think that if the Queen were to give him a responsible task, he would carry it out well."

The Archdeacon pursed his lips; the Prince's way of life was not approved by the godly. He said that he was glad to hear of the prospect of renewed fortune at Hubertshall, and in the circumstances understood that Anna Belinda could not undertake further responsibility. He enquired for Hubert, and was shown that young gentleman, tall and strong for his age, and inclined to be pert when asked if he knew his catechism. "When you go off to school, which I understand will be soon, they will make sure, by unfailing means, that you know it. It would be better to learn it now," the churchman said.

Mother and son saw him into his carriage, and watched him drive off; then Anna Belinda returned her gaze longingly to Hubert, of whom she saw increasingly little these days. It was true that she had always intended sending him to school when he was ready, but the time had passed so quickly! Only yesterday, it seemed to her, he had been a little child who clung to her; now, if he clung to anyone, it was to Gertrude Lumley. The fascination that woman had for children, and for men, was unaccountable. Even Zoë did what she was told, albeit in an ungracious manner; but Zoë was a conceited, unpleasant child, reminding one of the worst aspects of her mother Constance. It troubled Anna Belinda that she should share lessons with Hubert. Once she had spoken to Gertrude Lumley about it, and had been rewarded by a direct glance from the dark eyes, usually veiled by creamy lids.

"Hubert is lazy, I fear," said the

governess who was Lewis's mistress. "Zoë is clever and grasps at the least thing, and will soon catch up with Hubert if he is not careful. School will be the making of him."

So they were sending her son away. When he was gone, her life here would be empty of everything but misery. Yet she shuddered at the thought of going down to Vollands to be with Maud and the girls. There was her father to see to; that was the lifeline to which she clung; that and the books, which Lewis still went over with her monthly. And there were the guests to whom to look forward. She would be glad of the guests.

Preparations for them, or rather for the arrival of His Royal Highness, commenced well before the autumn, with the digging in of late-flowering shrubs and bedding plants, the hiring of beaters from all the countryside round; setting up of butts, cleaning out the lake which had grown foul, weeding the island; and, indoors, polishing the silver till it shone, waxing the woodwork and the floors, and making the windows sparkle. Later, there was the royal bedroom to be made ready; the linen aired, the fire laid, the bottle of whisky placed by the bedside; everything as A. E. was accustomed to it. Downstairs, the picnic hampers were unpacked from where they had lain in store; orders were placed for grouse and other delicacies, the ice-house in the well was inspected to ensure that the summer months had not impaired its coldness; an orchestra was hired to beguile the evening hours for those who did not want to play cards, and for those who did, there were tables ready. The billiard-room was dusted, the green baize uncovered and its level checked; darts were available in a further room, as even the ladies had been known to play at these. Outside, apart from the shooting, there was archery and croquet, the hoops sticking up out of the shaved grass already, waiting for the players. Everything, in short, was available to give the Prince and his companions a pleasant weekend; and Anna Belinda was exhausted.

But it was done; she had satisfied herself that everything was as it should be, and Lewis could have no possible complaint. It was particularly important that the Prince should be pleased; he had done this, she was fairly certain, to help bring back prosperity to Hubertshall after its late disaster. Peter Lumley was in prison, serving twelve years; it had been pleaded in mitigation that the Duke had attacked him and was in poor health, or else he might have been hanged for murder. Anna Belinda did not dwell on the question of what Peter would think of his wife's present conduct. She tried to put it out of her mind. Since Hubert had gone off to school in the previous week there was nothing for Gertrude to do except teach Zoë, but she had not offered to help in any way with the manifold tasks which had had to be carried out in time for the Prince's visit. Perhaps the governess knew of Anna Belinda's dislike, or perhaps — Anna Belinda admitted this wryly to herself — the dislike was mutual.

It was at this moment that she herself returned to James's room to find the man who should have been looking after him absent, and James dead, his mouth fallen open in the manner of corpses. The Prince was due to arrive on the following day.

"You cannot possibly have a coffin in the house during the Prince's visit. You must take the body out of here, to Vollands. The undertakers may get on with their business down there."

She heard Lewis speak as though he was a stranger, then realised that that was what he had always been; a cold, hard stranger, who cared nothing for her, who used her as a servant, who when she was no longer of value to him would cast her off, without pity. All this she knew; and yet still loved him, still understood what it meant to him to have this visit pass off without hindrance, such as a death.

He could not even spare the time to come with her in the carriage; he was busy at the butts, he insisted. So she sat alone with the body of James, covered by a sheet, swaying on the seat opposite, with the light outside growing dark. They got to Vollands as lamps were being lit. Beatrice and Adela, who had been warned of their coming, were waiting helplessly. There was no sign of Maud.

"Where are we to put him?" Beatrice asked. In the end the three of them carried the sheeted corpse into the ground-floor bedroom, laid it on the bed and left it there. Adela had begun to shiver violently. "Don't be a fool," said Beatrice.

A tumbling sound disturbed them from above; there was a confused cry. "It's Mother," said Adela, and began to run upstairs. Beatrice shrugged; they were used to varied noises from Maud. She went to the door to see Anna Belinda back into the carriage, when they heard Adela cry out.

"Mother's hurt herself. She's fallen downstairs. Please come."

They went up. Adela was kneeling, a lamp by her, beside the grotesque figure of Maud. The old woman had fallen downstairs, turning head over heels in the process; her neck was at an odd angle. She made no sound.

"Do you think she's — oh, do you think she's — "

"Be quiet," said Beatrice. "Someone had better fetch the doctor."

Anna Belinda waited till the doctor came, aware that Lewis would be angry at the delay. When the man arrived, she explained what had happened and that she could not wait. The Reverend Mark Volland was the person to be informed of both deaths. She knew that her mother was dead: had known as soon as she saw her. She drove back to Hubertshall in the carriage with her eyes closed in a blend of weariness and self-disgust. She had had to leave her sisters to deal with the double deaths alone; and Lewis would, she knew, forbid her emergence from the house in black to attend the funeral, lest the royal visit be inconvenienced.

The funeral took place. James and Maud Volland lay side by side at last in death as they had not done in life for many years. The small party of mourners walked away from the vault through the graveyard, many of whose stones were tilting and overgrown with lichen, their letters effaced. Jenny's were still clear.

The Archdeacon had Ellen on his arm. She was much troubled with rheumatism, and had not come to Maudie's funeral; but had made the effort to attend her sister's. Mark took great care of her; as a housekeeper she had been a resounding success, a martinet with the maids and standing no nonsense from parishioners who arrived on the doorstep to disturb him when he was busy. He wanted to keep her as long as possible; but the old died. He helped her into the waiting carriage, seeing above her stiff movements her hair, long turned white, below a bonnet with jet bugles. She no longer looked like a headmistress.

Behind them, Octavia Tillotson was talking to her nieces. "I think it is disgraceful that Anna Belinda was not present; after all she inherits everything James left. It would have shown respect for her father's memory." She bridled a little; although she herself was very well off as regarded worldly goods, it would have been appreciated if James had left her a little souvenir of some kind. After all, she was the only one of their generation left except Mark, who as a clergyman might be expected to be above worldly things.

She glanced at the two girls, pale as bone, shabbily dressed, and smelling a trifle even in the open air. "I have been thinking about you two," she said, "and you cannot remain alone at Vollands. You must come to me." Her sons, both of them, had for some years now been married to young women who owned separate estates, and although they saw that Octavia was not left unvisited, she would be glad of company other than that of the servants. The first thing to do would be to get Beatrice and Adela bathed and suitably gowned; after that, they could all live as they had been intended to do, in a civilised manner, with the county calling. She talked on persuasively as they went down the path between the graves, and by the time the iron gate was reached Beatrice and Adela, naturally obedient, were ready to do as they were told, without too much resentment in their own minds; after all, Surtees Hall was a good deal more comfortable than Vollands, even though Aunt Octavia would certainly arrange their lives.

"What will happen to the house?" Beatrice thought of asking.

"It will have to be shut up," replied Octavia firmly. "Anna Belinda owns it, and may decide for herself what to do with it. We will send her the key." She looked them over critically once again. "There is no point in your going back to a sad, empty house," she said. "You may as well come with me now in the carriage; your things can be sent on later." The things, she had already decided, had better be burned; she would replace them with others.

The royal weekend at Hubertshall had been a success, with a sizeable bag falling to His Royal Highness at the butts, superb autumn weather, and the evenings filled with music from the hired orchestra, which played quadrilles and waltzes. The Prince did not join in — he was already growing too stout to dance — but watched in satisfaction while the ladies, in elaborate coiffures and gowns from Paris, twirled and cavorted, assisted by the gentlemen, to the beat of the drums, flutes, and violins. Where, Albert Edward demanded, was the handsome woman who had been here last time? He then recalled that Constance had had her portrait taken, that that had been the cause of the scandal, and tactfully fell silent. Anna Belinda replied quietly that Mrs Hetherwick had returned to her husband and son.

"Lucky man," said the Prince, and gazed with his pale-blue, heavy-lidded eyes above Anna Belinda's head to where beauty was dancing. All that he required to make him happy, for the time, had been found here; a good place to have discovered, must come again! He nodded amiably at the woman who had made all this possible, as if to dismiss her; Anna Belinda was aware of the aroma of his cigars and the scent of lavender-water which he used. She curtseyed, and was about to withdraw; it was a silent evening, being Sunday, and no cards were played; but the click of billiard balls was permitted, and it was against the sound of these that the Prince spoke again.

"Here comes Crozier. Must thank him. I have to leave very early, you know, for an engagement at Goodwood tomorrow; may not see him again."

Anna Belinda turned, and saw Lewis advancing with, on his arm, Gertrude Lumley. The latter no longer wore dark dull clothes; she was as expensively attired as any, in a gown the colour of dead leaves which swirled with grace about her. Her dark hair was piled fashionably on top of her head, with a false front. She wore diamond earrings and, on her narrow wrists, diamonds flashed also.

"Allow me to present my wife to Your Royal Highness," Lewis said.

Anna Belinda stood as if turned to stone. She saw Gertrude make a full Court curtsey; no doubt about the background there! They talked, the three of them; the Prince, the proprietor and the bride. How could it have happened, with Lumley still in prison?

Nobody heeded Anna Belinda as she made her way out past the gossiping society women, the bent backs of the men over their billiard cues. She went along the passages to her own room, shut the door and gazed into the mirror, as if to banish from her mind the thing that had lately entered it. She stared at the colour of her dress, which was silver grey. Blue had seemed insipid, green needed a healthy colour she did not possess, yellow was out of the question, pink was frivolous. So she had chosen the silver grey; and it made her look like a ghost.

Reflected behind her was the dressing-table, and on it lay a letter. She turned about and went and tore it open. It was in Lewis's handwriting; she knew it well enough from the alterations he frequently made to her account books. In all these years, he had never written to her before.

My dear sister-in-law, — he could have used her Christian name; but almost certainly this had been shown to Gertrude and approved by her —

We are both sorry not to have informed you sooner of the marriage between us, which took place very privately last week. The reason for silence was the coming royal visit, which as you will understand meant that no scandal or gossip must again attach itself to Hubertshall. The fact is that, some weeks ago now, Peter Lumley killed himself in prison by cutting his wrists with a razor he had by some means acquired. We have had considerable trouble in keeping the affair out of the newspapers. However regrettable such an end may be, it left Gertrude free to marry me, and I need hardly say that we are most happy. I trust we have your good wishes.

I want to discuss with you the question of Hubert. Gertrude is unable to have children, and I should like to make him my heir: he is after all the son of my dear brother. This means that he would inherit all of Maria's fortune, her holdings in the northern coalfields and property in London which will have risen in value by the time he is of age and Hubertshall itself, which is now not inconsiderable as a country seat, if nothing else. I am also prepared to put him through preparatory school, public school, and Oxford. You will agree that all this gives him a chance in life that other young men would envy. I make one condition; he and Zoë must be married as soon as they are of age. I am responsible for her, and cannot give her a season such as other young girls have, because of her origins. On the other hand she may be presented as soon as she is married.

Gertrude agrees with me in the views expressed here, and I hope that you yourself will not oppose them. We will

313

of course be happy to have you here at Hubertshall for as long as you care to stay. I am grateful for all you have done to ensure that the venture is a success.

Your devoted brother-in-law,
Lewis Crozier

She tore the letter across and across. Her folly in doing so, in destroying any evidence of his offer to Hubert, did not trouble her; she was past trouble. He had used her, worked her to the bone, had betrayed her, had taken her son from her, had failed to trust her even in the late matter of Lumley's suicide. Happy to have her here for as long as she cared to stay! She would not stay a quarter-hour.

She found her woollen cloak, flung it about her, took the key of Vollands from its drawer in her desk and set out. The night was starry and she could see her way. She walked on, down the hill, up which she had so often driven in his carriage; there would be no more carriages. She heard the light sound of her feet on the road; the night had grown cold and the two-mile walk scarcely warmed her. She met no one on the way; the place was enveloped in silence, the wayside trees dark and still.

Vollands was dark also. She found the lock and fitted the key into it. It turned with difficulty, as if the short time the house had been left empty had been enough to make it rust. The door creaked open finally, inside it was dark, and her footsteps on the flagged passages had a dead, final sound. She passed through one room after another, coming at last to the kitchen; and in the grate was a little glow of fire.

She did not ask herself how it had come there, who had lit it and then left it. She huddled down by it and tried to fan it into flame. She searched about the hearth for sticks, twigs, anything to nourish the hint of warmth; the rest of the house was cold. By day, she would know where things were kept; she would not on any account go back to Hubertshall. She had never known bodily love, hardly known kindness. At her age they might not come; but there were other things.

She had begun to shiver; the illusion of warmth from the tiny glow was not enough. Her eyes had become accustomed to the objects in the room and she could see Mrs Anna's chaise-longue, banished long ago from the drawing-room and brought in here. Its stuffing was coming out. There would be a lot to do at Vollands. Fortunately she had her own money and could please herself, could employ servants and see that they did as she chose. She was no longer working for another. The thought of that still brought her pain, but the pain had dulled, as though her very breaking away had lanced a boil; she smiled wryly at the inelegant comparison.

There was a noise at the far side of the room and she thought it was a mouse, scraping at the woodwork. Then it grew louder. "Who is there?" she called. She was not afraid; nothing that could happen to her mattered any more. She turned her head and saw a man's tall form bend to admit him past the lintel of the door. "Who are you?" she said. "How did you get in?"

"I'm Jim. Don't be afeared. I got in by the hall window. I know how to unlatch it. You're cold, sitting there."

He came to the grate, knelt down,

took a box of paraffin matches from his trousers pocket, and made the fire start up; laying on little twigs one by one, till the blaze rose high. She could see his hawk's profile lit by the flames; and remembered, again, how she had told her father long ago that this was Uncle Hew's son and not his. How different everything would have been but for that! Tinker Jim would have been educated, presentable, a gentleman and rich. She owed him a lot; her money was his, after all.

"Did you mean to stay here?" she asked quietly.

"Ay, overnight. I stayed last night. I had something I wanted to fetch away. The others are in the north. They might be back for the winter, or they might not. They're with Thyrza's sister." He suddenly turned full face and looked at her. This wasn't a bitch, he was thinking, like Maudie had been. That was why he had kept Maudie under him, to still her tongue. This was a woman who wasn't like her sisters. She wasn't like anyone he had met before, come to that, except that time up at Hubertshall when he had been digging the plots, and they had spoken together.

"You're the lady of the house," he said. "We have to ask you if they can come back or not."

"I will think about it," Anna Belinda told him. She was still not warmed through. She said, "I should like a cup of tea."

"I've got better than tea, that'll warm you."

He rose, and she was aware of his great height and long limbs, also of a certain gentleness about him. She thought of her mother. "Not whisky," she said. "I don't want whisky. I should prefer tea."

"You give me a minute, and you'll not want tea again. This'll be better."

He went out, and a few minutes later came back with a large brimming jug and two tankards. He set them on the table and poured a foaming liquid out of the jug. She watched him curiously. Her mind seemed to have become obedient, with no will of its own; nothing that had happened, or would happen, mattered now. She knew she would drink whatever it was he had brought. It was a help to have him here for as long as he chose to stay. She thought of his departure with desolation. It was not only that he knew where things were, would show her, at least, how to begin this new way of living. At the back of her mind she realised that she had left all comforts, such as linen sheets, at Hubertshall. It didn't matter. She would never go back. But there was the nightmare of Julius to keep away.

Tinker Jim carried over a brimming tankard in each hand, balancing them carefully. "This is what I came back for," he said, "but it's better drunk here."

The bright dark eyes regarded her beneath their hooded lids. She accepted a tankard, holding it away from her dress. The pennyroyal beer foamed over the rim. Jim held his tankard against hers and the sides touched. They drank together while the fire blazed high, filling the room with shadows.

The carriage conveying A. E. to Goodwood bowled by in the dawn, as arranged. The two lying together did not hear him pass.

TO FIGHT THE WILD
Rod Ansell and Rachel Percy

Lost in uncharted Australian bush, Rod Ansell survived by hunting and trapping wild animals, improvising shelter and using all the bushman's skills he knew.

COROMANDEL
Pat Barr

India in the 1830s is a hot, uncomfortable place, where the East India Company still rules. Amelia and her new husband find themselves caught up in the animosities which seethe between the old order and the new.

THE SMALL PARTY
Lillian Beckwith

A frightening journey to safety begins for Ruth and her small party as their island is caught up in the dangers of armed insurrection.

SKINWALKERS
Tony Hillerman

The peace of the land between the sacred mountains is shattered by three murders. Is a 'skinwalker', one who has rejected the harmony of the Navajo way, the murderer?

A PARTICULAR PLACE
Mary Hocking

How is Michael Hoath, newly arrived vicar of St. Hilary's, to meet the demands of his flock and his strained marriage? Further complications follow when he falls hopelessly in love with a married parishioner.

A MATTER OF MISCHIEF
Evelyn Hood

A saga of the weaving folk in 18th century Scotland. Physician Gavin Knox was desperately seeking a cure for the pox that ravaged the slums of Glasgow and Paisley, but his adored wife, Margaret, stood in the way.

THE SONG OF THE PINES
Christina Green

Taken to a Greek island as substitute for David Nicholas's secretary, Annie quickly falls prey to the island's charms and to the charms of both Marcus, the Greek, and David himself.

GOODBYE DOCTOR GARLAND
Marjorie Harte

The story of a woman doctor who gave too much to her profession and almost lost her personal happiness.

DIGBY
Pamela Hill

Welcomed at courts throughout Europe, Kenelm Digby was the particular favourite of the Queen of France, who wanted him to be her lover, but the beautiful Venetia was the mainspring of his life.

LEAVE IT TO THE HANGMAN
Bill Knox

Dope, dynamite, guns, currency — whatever it was John Kilburn and his son Pat had known how to get it in or out of England, if the price was right. But their luck changed when one of them killed a cop.

A VIOLENT END
Emma Page

To Chief Inspector Kelsey there was no shortage of suspects when Karen Boland was murdered, and that was before he discovered that she stood to inherit substantially at twenty-one.

SILENCE IN HANOVER CLOSE
Anne Perry

In 1884 Robert York is found brutally murdered at his home in Hanover Close. When, three years later, Inspector Pitt is asked to investigate, the murder remains unsolved.

PREJUDICED WITNESS
Dilys Gater

Fleur Rowley finds when she leaves London for her 'author's retreat' in the wilds of North Wales that she is drawn, in spite of herself, into an old tragedy.

GENTLE TYRANT
Lucy Gillen

Working as Ross McAdam's secretary, Laura couldn't imagine why his bitchy ex-wife should see her as a rival.

DEAR CAPRICE
Juliet Gray

Clifford Fortune married Caprice but his brother, Luke, knew the marriage was a mistake. He could allow himself to love Caprice blindly but that would be betraying his own brother.

BALLET GENIUS
Gillian Freeman and Edward Thorpe

Presents twenty pen portraits of great dancers of the twentieth century and gives an insight into their daily lives, their professional careers, the ever present risk of injury and the pressure to stay on top.

TO LIVE IN PEACE
Rosemary Friedman

The final part of the author's Anglo-Jewish trilogy, which began with PROOFS OF AFFECTION and ROSE OF JERICHO, telling the story of Kitty Shelton, widowed after a happy marriage, and her three children.

NORA WAS A NURSE
Peggy Gaddis

Nurse Nora Courtney was hopelessly in love with Doctor Owen Baird and when beautiful Lillian Halstead set her cap for him, Nora realised she must make him see her as a desirable woman as well as an efficient nurse.

DEATH TRAIN
Robert Byrne

The tale of a freight train out of control and leaking a paralytic nerve gas that turns America's West into a scene of chemical catastrophe in which whole towns are rendered helpless.

THE ADVENTURE OF THE CHRISTMAS PUDDING
Agatha Christie

In the introduction to this short story collection the author wrote "This book of Christmas fare may be described as 'The Chef's Selection'. I am the Chef!"

RETURN TO BALANDRA
Grace Driver

Returning to her Caribbean island home, Suzanne looks forward to being with her parents again, but most of all she longs to see Wim van Branden, a coffee planter she has known all her life.

A GREAT DELIVERANCE
Elizabeth George

Into the web of old houses and secrets of Keldale Valley comes Scotland Yard Inspector Thomas Lynley and his assistant to solve a particularly savage murder.

'E' IS FOR EVIDENCE
Sue Grafton

Kinsey Millhone was bogged down on a warehouse fire claim. It came as something of a shock when she was accused of being on the take. She'd been set up. Now she had a new client — herself.

A FAMILY OUTING IN AFRICA
Charles Hampton and Janie Hampton

A tale of a young family's journey through Central Africa by bus, train, river boat, lorry, wooden bicycle and foot.

MORNING IS BREAKING
Lesley Denny

The growing frenzy of war catapults Diane Clements into a clandestine marriage and separation with a German refugee.

LAST BUS TO WOODSTOCK
Colin Dexter

A girl's body is discovered huddled in the courtyard of a Woodstock pub, and Detective Chief Inspector Morse and Sergeant Lewis are hunting a rapist and a murderer.

THE STUBBORN TIDE
Anne Durham

Everyone advised Carol not to grieve so excessively over her cousin's death. She might have followed their advice if the man she loved thought that way about her, but another girl came first in his affections.

THE LISTERDALE MYSTERY
Agatha Christie

Twelve short stories ranging from the light-hearted to the macabre, diverse mysteries ingeniously and plausibly contrived and convincingly unravelled.

TO BE LOVED
Lynne Collins

Andrew married the woman he had always loved despite the knowledge that Sarah married him for reasons of her own. So much heartache could have been avoided if only he had known how vital it was to be loved.

ACCUSED NURSE
Jane Converse

Paula found herself accused of a crime which could cost her her job, her nurse's reputation, and even the man she loved, unless the truth came to light.

THE TWILIGHT MAN
Frank Gruber

Jim Rand lives alone in the California desert awaiting death. Into his hermit existence comes a teenage girl who blows both his past and his brief future wide open.

DOG IN THE DARK
Gerald Hammond

Jim Cunningham breeds and trains gun dogs, and his antagonism towards the devotees of show spaniels earns him many enemies. So when one of them is found murdered, the police are on his doorstep within hours.

THE RED KNIGHT
Geoffrey Moxon

When he finds himself a pawn on the chessboard of international espionage with his family in constant danger, Guy Trent becomes embroiled in moves and countermoves which may mean life or death for Western scientists.